JAN JONES

AN ORDINARY GIFT

Complete and Unabridged

LINFORD
Leicester

First published in Great Britain in 2015

First Linford Edition
published 2017

A catalogue record for this book is available
from the British Library.

ISBN 978–1–4448–3147–4

Published by
F. A. Thorpe (Publishing)
Anstey, Leicestershire

Set by Words & Graphics Ltd.
Anstey, Leicestershire
Printed and bound in Great Britain by
T. J. International Ltd., Padstow, Cornwall

This book is printed on acid-free paper

AN ORDINARY GIFT

New job. New town. New house. Everything Clare needs for a fresh start. She could do without the ghosts, though ... Determined to put an unhappy love affair behind her, Clare moves to Ely in the Cambridgeshire Fens to catalogue an early music library. But why does the house she rents in this ancient city feel so familiar? Who is singing Gregorian chants that only she can hear? And what can she do about her growing attraction to Ewan, the site manager of the library, when neither wants a rebound relationship?

Books by Jan Jones
in the Linford Romance Library:

FAIRLIGHTS

An Ordinary Gift

is dedicated to my writing friends

Louise Allen, who told me the
original was too short
and**Lesley Cookman,** who kept
nagging me for 'the Ely story'

Acknowledgements

Any mistakes are my own,
but I owe thanks to

The City of Ely museum and
visitor information centre

Ely Cathedral

Toppings of Ely, bookshop
extraordinaire, for inspiring my
fictional library

and you, if I've
forgotten to include you

1

As soon as I saw the house in Almoner's Place, I knew I'd made the right choice. I felt my chest ease, felt my worries loosen. Yes, this move was about me and taking my life back and making a fresh start, but oh, it was going to be so much easier in a house that, even before I'd stepped inside, already felt like home.

I hugged myself in delight at the sheer age of the house. No. 4 Almoner's Place was so old that its brickwork was almost featureless. It grew out of the street, breathing permanence, leaning against its neighbour like a pregnant woman bracing her hip against the bus stop after a long day. It was narrow at the top, with square windows under a dipped roofline, swelling outwards to bulge comfortably at the ground floor. The window recesses were shallow. There was barely any clearance between the lowest sills and the sloping line of the ancient lane. The whole feel of the house said it had withstood sun and rain, feast and famine, riots in the streets and slumbering years of peace. It was anchored in time and it would anchor me.

I smiled gently. I could see myself living here. I could see my sheets on the bed, my bright pans in the kitchen, and my collection of tiny cats on the windowsill. The last pain-filled weeks — the decision to step away from Jonathan and take this quiet, academic job, miles from his busy city life; putting distance between us and restoring the dignity I'd once had . . . none of it mattered now. All would be well.

At the far end of the lane, the cab that had brought me from Ely station drove off. My journey was now in the past, a lifetime away. I knew this process well. It had been the same throughout my growing up. Every time we'd moved to a new parish, taken on a new church challenge, and settled into a different vicarage, my father had said, 'The secret is to keep the past in mind, Clare, but remember the present. *This* is the life that counts, right now.'

Right now, at this moment, meant collecting the keys to No. 4 Almoner's Place and making it mine. I sent the house a silent promise that I would be with it soon, and transferred my attention to the building next door.

No.s 1–3 Almoner's Place was square-on to the pavement, and had three times the frontage of No. 4 and much fresher paint. It was a familiar address to anyone involved with the collection or study of early music. Time and again when Jonathan had been bidding on a manuscript, either for a client or speculating for the firm, he'd been beaten by a telephone bid from Dr Leonard Smith, Almoner's Place, Ely. Even before I came within Jon's orbit, back in the days when I was still a research student existing on grants, compassion and fresh air, I'd spend weeks tracking down the particular folio I needed, only to find that it was in Almoner's Place and thus out of reach.

Dr Leonard Smith himself was not a man to be taken lightly. He was elderly, yes. He was irascible, certainly. He was also the most eminent academic I knew in the field of early music. His breadth of knowledge was legendary, but as Jon pointed out with an increasingly contemplative gleam in his eye, the man couldn't keep spending on rare manuscripts forever. The crunch had come earlier this year. A whispered rumour had sprung up, then another, then a whole forest of speculation. The bank was moving in, the Bodleian was raising a subscription, the choicest pieces were going to Sotheby's to pay off debts . . .

In the event, Leonard confounded everyone. Rather than sell his treasures piecemeal to the collectors circling his assets, he struck a breathtaking deal with the Newrigg Foundation. Leonard would remain as curator, but Newrigg would take on 1–3 Almoner's Place, its maintenance and all the administration. Newrigg would ensure that the collection remained intact and provide the funds for Leonard to continue with his passion.

The sting in the tail was that the Newrigg Foundation was an institution with fiercely philanthropic, egalitarian principles. The price for their magnificent rescue was to make the entire collection available for study by bona fide academics and researchers. For that, their immediate need was for an archivist with up-to-the-minute IT skills, plus the sort of muted but irrefutable academic record acceptable to Leonard himself.

Me.

I have never been so glad in my life of my father's early habit of lending me out for library work to his ecclesiastical contacts during my vacations. He, being a career vicar with an eye to a mitre, had been doing it for his own advancement, but his networking by proxy had stood me in good stead. It had got me into some of the greatest early music collections in the country and given me an unimpeachable CV. The knowledge within those libraries had got me my degree, my PhD, and my travelling research scholarship around Europe.

I had then blown it spectacularly by meeting Jonathan in Florence when I was dizzy with music and architecture, falling stupidly in love with him, and spending the next five years working in the technical department of Jonathan Ambergris Fine Art & Music and waiting for it to be the right time for him to leave his wife.

The news of the Newrigg Foundation archivist position had hit the ether on the same day that Jonathan's wife Marianne had burst joyously into the office with the news that she was expecting their third child. They had gone into the most massive spontaneous delighted clinch in front of the whole team. I'd shut my door, rung Newrigg Head Office there and then, applied for the post over the phone, and got an interview the next day.

I'm not sure, even then, whether I would have gone ahead with it had Jon not come into my office later and acted as if nothing had changed. As it was, I was able to tell the Newrigg directors with perfect truth that I wanted this job with all my heart and that there was no bar to me moving to Ely as soon as possible for as long as the cataloguing might take, be it weeks, months or years.

The Newrigg Foundation approved of my industry experience (I heard one of the directors murmur that I'd need it). The interview board also strongly approved of my ecclesiastical background. Dr Leonard Smith wasn't present, but he presumably looked at my emailed CV and saw me as less of a threat than any of the other applicants. I was called back to Head Office within twenty-four hours, signed the contract, and came away with half a tree's worth of Visions, Aims and Ideals and instructions as to how it was all going to work. The meeting with Jonathan when I tendered my resignation was a lot less smooth.

My father had been overjoyed with the news of my career change. At last I would be back in academe. Back where I could be a Useful Daughter. And in Ely, too, with its rich source of influential clergy. He'd immediately bustled off to open a bottle of the good red in celebration.

My mother was less sanguine. 'This job is in Ely?' she said, fluffing up her hair, the same unusual pale blonde shade as my own, and shooting me an anxious glance in the mirror. 'Really, darling? Ely? Are you quite sure you should take it?'

Dad was burrowing into the far reaches of the cupboard under the stairs, where he kept the better wine away from the predations of divinity students and visiting curates. I dropped my voice so he wouldn't hear. 'I need to get away from London.'

'I know *that*,' she said, and gave my arm a tiny squeeze. 'None too soon, if you ask me. Which you haven't, of course, and I would never dream of interfering. But Clare, you hate Ely.'

I stopped in the act of getting out the glasses. 'I don't hate Ely. How can I? I've never been there.'

'Yes you have, darling.'

'No I haven't. I think I'd remember.'

'It was years ago. You can only have been seven or eight. We were on our way to visit the cathedral there — we were within sight of it actually; it's got this huge great tower that looms up at the end of the street — when you suddenly started screaming that this was a horrible, horrible place. You went on and on.'

I felt embarrassed, as one does when told of something unreasonable one did as a child. 'I don't remember that at all. What did you do?'

'Not a lot we could do, with the noise you were making. We went back to the car and drove to the cathedral at Bury

St Edmunds instead.'

'Gosh. Sorry,' I said belatedly.

'Oh, I didn't mind. It was market day in Bury St Edmunds and the shops were excellent. I'm going to put extra helpings on your plate, darling; you've got much too thin. How old is this Dr Leonard Smith?'

'Older than Dad,' I said. 'Sorry again.'

She took it philosophically. 'Oh well, I'm glad about the new job anyway.'

★ ★ ★

So. My new life. I took a deep breath and hauled on the bell pull of No.s 1–3 Almoner's Place. There were sounds from inside. A shout and a response. The door was answered by a man of roughly my own age with hazel eyes, a tangle of messy dark hair that looked as though it had once been a smart crop, a light powdering of plaster dust, and an air of unobtrusive authority. In the background I could hear hammering

10

and a shouted conversation.

'Hi,' I said. 'Sorry to bother you, but I'm Clare Somerset. I'm starting work here tomorrow, cataloguing the early music collection, and I'm renting No. 4 from the Newrigg Foundation as of today. I was told to call here for the keys.' As I said the words, I could feel the tug of the next-door house. Longing glowed in me, causing me to treat the man to a much warmer smile than I'd normally bestow on a new acquaintance.

He was startled into smiling back at me. He had a pleasant, clever face, sensible rather than conventionally handsome. 'Dr Somerset. Do come in. Head Office emailed me about the lease. Just to warn you, the house is a recent acquisition, and it's been redecorated and left simply furnished, but not much else. You knew that, yes? I'm the site manager, Ewan Matlock. Leave your case in the hall for now; it'll be easier. I've got the keys in my office. I just need you to sign for them and you're ready to go.'

The site manager? He must be good, then, to be managing an old-buildings project in his early thirties. 'Thank you,' I said. 'I only use *Dr* if I think people aren't taking me seriously. I usually answer to Clare.'

Ewan Matlock's slow smile was a killer. 'That's grand. We're all on first-name terms here. I'll introduce you to the rest of the guys tomorrow. Leonard's upstairs in the library, but I don't think there's any point disturbing him until you actually clock on in the morning. The staff kitchen and usual offices are down the hall on the left-hand side. Everywhere else on the ground floor is in a bit of a state.'

'I can see that,' I said, glancing through open doors at ladders, cables, men discussing blueprints, stacks of sawn timber, and a laptop with graphs running across the screen. 'What are you actually doing?' I caught sight of my reflection in a snatch of mirror, all blue eyes and pale hair, and hurriedly shook my hair forward to cover the sharp points of my collarbones. *New life*, I reminded myself. I'd start with large meals. Or indeed, any.

'It's more a case of what *aren't* we doing,' Ewan said. 'Primarily, we're building new housing for the collection. At the same time, we're checking the state of the walls, the beams, the floors, the ceilings, putting in twenty-first century plumbing, rewiring throughout; and once I'm sure it's not going to blow up on us, we'll be adding a very, very fancy alarm system. Everything has been shifted upstairs to the library while we concentrate down here. I don't fancy the job you'll have cataloguing it all.'

We reached Ewan's office, tiny but methodical, with a mad mixture of furniture obviously salvaged from the house. 'Here you go,' he said, unlocking a bureau that wouldn't have looked out of place in an Edwardian study. He pulled out a bunch of antique keys and a sheaf of Newrigg Foundation paper.

'Sign here, please.' Then he paused, the ring of keys swinging from his finger. I sensed an odd reluctance to pass them over. He shook his head and dropped them with a solid jangle into my hand. 'My mobile is on twenty-four hours. I've left the number next door on the table. Let me know if there are any problems.'

'What sort of problems?' I queried.

Again there was just a trace of discomfort. 'Normal old-house stuff. Anything really. Electricity cutting out, water not heating up, doors jamming . . . You didn't bring a car?'

'No, I've been living in central London so I haven't needed one.'

'Just as well. There's no parking. Central London — you'll be saving a fortune on rent then.'

I let my hair swing forward again. 'It was a very small flat,' I mumbled, not mentioning that Jonathan had found it for me and insisted on subsidising it because it was handy for the office.

Ewan showed me to the front door.

In his top pocket, I heard his phone start ringing. 'The shops are mostly off to the left,' he said, fishing it out. 'There's a supermarket up in the Cloisters. We didn't get anything in for you, I'm afraid. Hello, Ewan Matlock speaking.'

I smiled at the tactful dismissal. This was a busy man. 'I didn't expect anything,' I said. 'Thanks for all the help. I'll see you tomorrow.'

Outside, I paused for a moment on the pavement, savouring the clean tang of the Cambridgeshire air and the bustling summer sounds of this small cathedral city, then I laid the palm of my hand flat against the wall of my new home. It was something I'd always done, every time my family had moved to a new vicarage. It may sound silly, but I thought of it as introducing myself to the house so I wouldn't be a stranger when I walked through the door. Asking for a blessing, perhaps.

The wall of No. 4 was warm and rich with age. I realised with surprise, and with a strange rumble of reproach deep inside me, that I'd missed this. I'd missed the physical sense of a house. I'd been so overloaded with antiquity on my return from Europe that it had been a relief to move into the bland, characterless 1980s shoebox near Jonathan's office. I'd needed the respite, but I hadn't noticed how plain my life had become since then, not until now when I had six hundred years of history warming my palm. 'Thank you,' I said to the house, 'I needed that.'

No. 4 exuded a placid serenity back at me. I selected the front door key from the ring and turned it in the lock. The door opened smoothly. I walked in, leant my case against the reception counter, put my handbag and shoulder tote on the desk, and turned automatically to hang my jacket on the row of hooks behind the door.

And stopped dead, an icy shiver streaking up my spine.

I knew where everything was when I walked in.

I had never been in this house before, never even read a description of it. Nothing outside on the street suggested that No. 4 Almoner's Place wasn't completely residential — yet between laying my hand on the wall and stepping across the threshold, I had *known* I would walk in on a working room with a swept floor, a tall mahogany counter, a desk, and workbench. And a row of coat hooks on the wall.

I stood there, my hand frozen in the act of hanging my jacket on one of those curly black pegs. I was so stunned and so completely still that I could feel the individual threads of my linen jacket against my fingertips. I completed the act of dropping the jacket loop over the hook and turned slowly. 'Okay,' I said aloud, raising my voice to hear it over the pounding in my ears, 'it must have been in a brochure. I must have seen a photo. Maybe this room was in one of those slideshows on the internet when I was looking up Ely.'

Or perhaps there had been a photo on the wall at Newrigg Head Office where I'd had my interview. There had been one of No.s 1–3 Almoner's Place, I was sure of it, trumpeting the new acquisition. But would a rapidly seen photo have made such an impression? Would my knowledge be this specific? I swallowed, aware that I had *expected* the open fireplace to my right. And in the far wall was a door I was certain led to a kitchen. That wouldn't have shown up in a photo.

I swivelled to the left. Another door.

My chill of unease grew deeper. I might even have whimpered. It looked like a cupboard door, but my bones were whispering 'staircase'. I walked across to it, wanting to be wrong, willing the door to reveal shelves where I could keep books and stationery. It opened instead — as I had known it would — onto a set of narrow stairs curling upwards in the gap between this wall and the one connecting it to next door.

The hairs on the back of my neck rose. How had I known? How could I possibly ever have known that? As I gripped the handle, scared to my soul, a sensible voice in my head said, *Television, you idiot girl. Books. All those programmes you watched and the tomes you leafed through when you were going out with that architecture student.*

I let my lungs suck in air and allowed my heart to resume a steady beat. I didn't believe the sensible voice, not really; but as a reason not to grab my luggage and run screaming out of the front door towards the nearest hotel, it would do.

The house was friendly, I knew it was. I'd felt welcome from the first moment of seeing it. The scare it had given me just now wasn't its fault. It had been caused by some lingering *something* in my mind.

I exhaled. I still wanted to stay. I still

wanted to live here, unexplained fore-knowledge or not. I stepped through the not-cupboard door onto the uncar-peted treads of the staircase and was rewarded by my new home wrapping its aura around me as snugly as the walls hugged the stairwell. It was the most astonishingly comforting sensation.

The first floor held a living room with sofa, armchair, and a coffee table. A bedroom opened off it. I peered in: small and plain, a guest room or for storage. Nice enough, but it didn't speak to me. I ascended again via a second cupboard/stairway, emerging in a low-ceilinged, narrow bedroom. It had a double bed and carved wooden ottoman at one end, and a neat wardrobe and chest of drawers at the other. I laughed for sheer joy. This room was exactly as it should be. Even the tiny modern bathroom at the far end didn't raise any stabs of discord. It was perfect and it was mine and I loved it.

I hadn't expected Ely Cathedral to fill the window like it did: a dramatic reminder, in the way it wasn't at ground level, of just how much the cathedral had shaped the life and existence of this town. But that too was comforting. I would have to read up about it. I couldn't look out at something so close every day without knowing its history.

As I unpacked, I heard noises from next door. Tiny knocks and bumps. Faint voices. Presumably that would be the workmen, or maybe even Leonard Smith in his library. Even so, it was quieter than my London flat, where I'd been able to hear other people's lives from all directions twenty-four hours a day.

I hadn't known what the dress code would be for working here, so I'd packed two of everything for safety's sake until the rest of my luggage arrived during the week. Now I hung the last softly draping skirt up in the wardrobe and turned to make the bed.

I frowned, looking around. That was odd. The sheets, pillowcases, and duvet cover I'd put ready were nowhere to be seen. The room wasn't large enough to miss them. Had I carried them into the bathroom with my towels? I checked. They weren't there either.

I stood in the doorway between bathroom and bedroom, thoroughly puzzled. I let my eyes move slowly across the room. My gaze rested on the carved chest at the foot of the bed. It would be an obvious place to keep bedding. I lifted the lid.

Cedarwood and lavender spread upwards in a scented cloud. The interior of the chest was empty — except for my sheets, pillowcases, and duvet cover reposing neatly on a brown paper liner at the bottom.

But I hadn't put them there. This was the first time I'd opened the chest.

Just for a second — just for a tiny, fleeting whisker of a moment — I heard a stifled giggle. Then it was gone.

2

I have frequently found that the easiest way to resolve a worrying situation is to go shopping. It gives me something practical to concentrate on. It stops my mind spinning. Today, shopping for groceries was particularly calming. It's impossible to build awkward thoughts about carnivorous wooden chests into any kind of nightmare when you are calculating what size bag of potatoes will get you through to the end of the week and trying to remember if there was a freezer in the kitchen or just an icebox.

By the time I'd reached the bread aisle, I'd decided I would simply accept the house as it was. The strangeness was very strange indeed, but I'd swear on Dad's bible that those had been giggles I'd heard. Evil spirits do not giggle. Besides, I *knew*

Almoner's Place was benign.

The weather was pleasantly warm. The everyday weight of the shopping bag on my arm was soothing as I strolled back. I tried to analyse the feel of the town. It was at once very English, with the sense of having grown out of the land, but at the same time it had continental overtones, presumably from pilgrims and travellers from abroad in medieval times putting their stamp on the street architecture.

I wasn't concerned at all about getting lost, not with the cathedral as a giant landmark. As I'd noticed on the train, it could be seen from the next county, so the muddle of streets nearby presented no problems. I headed towards it, coming out of a narrow alley into a row of shops that I hadn't yet been along. I glanced around, orienting myself, and was distracted by noticing a narrow triangle of grass complete with . . . I blinked. Complete with a cannon. Why on earth would there be a cannon near the cathedral?

Intrigued, I walked across.

Suddenly, out of nowhere, I was overcome by horrible, endless cold. My feet were grafted to the pavement. I couldn't move, couldn't talk, could barely breathe. Sounds were deadened, scents highlighted. Far, far away I could hear an appalled voice whispering *No, no, no* . . . People passed either side of me but I was unable to reach out to them, unable to walk on. It was utterly terrifying.

'Dr Somerset? Clare? *Clare!*'

Someone shook my shoulder, breaking the dreadful paralysis. I stumbled against a man with messy dark hair and a worried expression.

'Thank you,' I gasped, recognising Ewan Matlock from the Newrigg Foundation.

'Are you all right?' he asked. 'What happened? You looked dreadful.'

I gave a convulsive shiver. 'Sorry. I, er, froze. Someone must have walked over my grave.' It was more than that, I knew. The icy void that had touched me had had nothing to do with any cosy cliché. It had been scary.

Perhaps fortunately, Ewan showed no signs of believing me. He relieved me of my shopping and turned me firmly in the opposite direction. 'If you were one of Dad's patients, he'd prescribe hot sweet tea. Come on, I'll walk you back. It won't take a moment. I've finished for the day anyway.'

'Thank you,' I said shakily. 'Your father's a doctor?' It wasn't that I wanted to know. It was to stop me thinking of that horrible void, that fearsome cold, the terror.

'He's a GP. It was a huge relief to him when I went in for civil engineering instead of medicine.'

Ewan continued to talk in a pleasant, anodyne way. Above us, the sun had shifted towards evening. People were walking past, chattering, heading home. I began to feel normal again.

'Will you be okay now?' He stood to one side while I unlocked the door.

The ring of keys was awkward. I

detached the front door one for my purse for everyday and took the rest through to the kitchen. 'Yes, thank you,' I said, hooking the ring over a nail hammered into the beam above the back door. 'I'll make myself that tea you prescribed.'

I turned to see Ewan looking startled. 'Astonishing,' he said, putting my shopping on the table and staring up at the blackened beam. 'I organised the refitting of this kitchen and never realised that nail was there.'

My stomach dropped as I followed his gaze. Neither had I realised it was there. I'd hung up the keys automatically, on a nail that I was now aware had been used for the same purpose for generations. I swallowed, feeling icy again, and groped for the edge of the table. How had I known? *How?*

Ewan must have thought I was about to faint. He was across the kitchen in two strides, pulling out a chair for me.

'Tea for sure,' I said, managing a smile. Then, because I couldn't help myself, I added plaintively, 'Ewan, is there something about this house I should know?'

He scrubbed a hand through his hair and sat down opposite me. 'Yes. No. Maybe. No. 4 was bought by the Foundation partly for security reasons, because it butts against next door, and partly so visiting directors could use it as a company flat. When we were refitting the kitchen, we kept finding tools not quite where we'd left them. We went through two microwaves before deciding to eat next door at lunchtimes. And then the Finance Director spent just one night here before changing his mind, saying the collection could do with the extra space. There was an architect here a couple of weeks ago talking about knocking through. That would be a whole new nightmare for me, I can tell you, so I was delighted when they told me you were renting it instead.'

Despite the weird stuff, my heart felt as if it was being wrenched from my body at these words. 'Oh no! They wouldn't really break through the walls, would they? That would be dreadful. It's so perfect. Is that the reason why the ground floor is set up as an office?'

'It was like that already. I told you we'd only done a superficial furnishing job. This was a shop when Newrigg bought it, with living quarters above. Those fittings are real Victorian mahogany, I'll have you know, not reproduction. It's always been the mercantile area of the town around here. Sorry, I should have warned you. It must have been a shock to open the front door and see a shop instead of a conventional hallway.'

But it *hadn't* surprised me — that had been the shock. 'Actually, it didn't,' I confessed. I met his eyes. 'I suppose this house has never been in a film or on television?'

'I've no idea. Why?'

I shook my head. 'I've been having *déjà vu* ever since I walked in.'

'Like with the nail?' He was quick,

I'll give him that.

'Not just the nail. I knew where *everything* was, and where the doors led to, and . . . ' I stopped short of telling him how my sheets had been put away for me. No need to confirm the impression that I was a complete basket case. 'Don't get me wrong — I love the house, and I'm not going to run out on either it or the job, especially as I've signed the lease for a year. But it would be nice to understand.'

He stood up. 'I can't help with understanding, but strangely enough, I don't disbelieve you. I know it sounds completely daft, but I've worked several times with surveyors who instinctively avoid faults or watercourses even before they've studied the terrain. They get a feeling for a place. I'm never judgmental about unexplained events now.'

I smiled wanly. 'Thanks for not suggesting the local psychiatrist. I'd hate to get a weird reputation before I've even started the job.'

'No worries. Look, are you all right

making tea and so forth?'

'I'll be fine. I need to ring Mum and reassure her I've penetrated the east of England with no ill effects. Families are great for bringing you back down to earth. I'm pretty sure I'm still fourteen years old in her eyes.'

He grinned. 'I know what you mean. Okay, I'll get off. See you tomorrow.'

Ewan left. I made tea and a plate of sandwiches, too weary now for anything more. I did ring Mum and tell her I'd got here okay, but I didn't mention finding the cold spot. I had forgotten, until that moment, her telling me I hated Ely. If something like that had happened back when I was a child, I'm not surprised I yelled. As it was, all I wanted was a bath and an early night, not a cosy hour-long conversation on how I'd always been a bit on the sensitive side. I also didn't mention Ewan Matlock when she fished for information on my new colleagues. For one thing, it would be a while before I was over Jonathan. For another, I had no idea about Ewan's personal circumstances. I did tell her I'd found a branch of Waitrose within walking distance. There was a thoughtful silence before she asked if the house had a spare room.

I turned off the lights as I went upstairs to bed, savouring the feel of handrails and stair-treads worn smooth with countless years' use. Around me, I felt the house settle for the night. None of it was in the least disturbing.

As I slid between my cool, clean sheets, I heard a Gregorian plainsong coming from next door. The beautiful notes reminded me that I must take up singing again. The cathedral would know of local choirs. *Lovely*, I thought sleepily, as pure treble voices wove themselves into my dreams.

★ ★ ★

Next morning I woke up to sunlight. I stretched happily. Almoner's Place already felt like home. I made tea and toast and took them into the 'shop' so I could eat at the counter and watch the goings-on outside through the square-paned, heavily leaded windows. The lane was evidently used as a cut-through to the High Street, judging by the few hurrying people, but there were also the workmen for next door arriving. I didn't see Ewan. Possibly he was at work already, or maybe he came towards the house from the other end of the lane.

I left my crockery on the side of the sink, checked my make-up and hair, and smoothed down my skirt. I didn't want to give a bad impression on my first day of a new job. Ewan, bless him, just happened to be holding a conversation with a couple of carpenters in the hallway as I nervously keyed in the entrance code he'd given me and walked inside.

'Morning,' he said cheerfully, quite as if he hadn't witnessed me doing some sort of Lady of Shallot act in the middle of Palace Green yesterday. He turned to the others and raised his voice over the noise of the refitting. 'Guys, this is Dr Clare Somerset. She's going to be working with Leonard. I'll take you up, shall I?'

The guys — there were perhaps six or seven of them — briefly stopped what they were doing and appeared through various doorways to chorus a hello.

'Hi,' I said, and to Ewan, 'That would be lovely, if you don't mind.'

He gave that delicious smile of his. 'I don't mind at all. I want to see your face when you see the collection for the first time.'

I frowned. What did he mean? Oh well, I'd find out soon enough.

'The library is all on the first floor,' he said. 'The second floor is Leonard's flat and more storage.'

At the top of the stairs was a narrow passage. Ewan stood back from an ordinary deal door, much like my internal doors in No. 4, and motioned for me to turn the handle. Hazel flecks positively danced in his eyes.

Bracing myself for whatever I might find, I opened the door to the library — and gasped as I stepped into an Aladdin's cave of panelled interconnecting rooms, each one crammed with bookcases, filing cabinets and tables. The whole glorious space was overflowing with the literary version of a dragon's hoard.

I turned once, to look in wonder at Ewan. He grinned again, mouthed *Told you*, and closed the door, leaving me in what must surely be the earthly aspect of Elysium. I stayed where I was, strung taut in exquisite pleasure, fixing this beautiful place in my memory for all time.

Sunlight slanted at intervals through narrow sash windows. It fell in square-patterned shafts onto piled manuscripts, folios, crinkled parchment and sheets of music. The labyrinth of rooms was research-quiet; immeasurably soothing after the busyness of the building work downstairs. It smelled of old wood and old ink and took me back a dozen years to Oxford, to when I was thirsty for academic knowledge and thought there was nothing else of life to learn. Standing here, breathing in the past, I knew I'd been foolish to worry about taking this job. This was my home. This was a scholar's place. The abysmal waste of the last five years of my life crowed loudly in my ears.

I trod softly between the tables, awed and delighted by the cloth- and leather-bound bounty piled up around me, amazed by the multiplicity of treasures just *lying*, inviting the unwary to pick them up and become immediately lost. I lifted the cover of a gold-embossed folio, hardly daring to breathe. Jewel-bright illustrations leapt out at me: a cat, a fox, a slithering serpent, as clear as when some long ago monk had inked the notes and thought to embellish the words for the greater glory of God. I shut it with infinite care, caught between exhilaration and a great sense of continuity.

'And you are?'

I jumped. A spare, colourless man with an impatient edge to his tone was standing in one of the inner doorways. Dr Leonard Smith. I walked forward, extending my hand. 'I'm Dr Clare Somerset. I'm delighted to meet you, Dr Smith. We've talked on the phone and I've attended several of your talks at conferences. I'm here to catalogue the collection.' I looked around and couldn't help adding, 'I may never leave.'

His lips thinned. 'I've always said I'll do it one day. It isn't as if I don't know exactly what I've got and where everything is.'

But no one else would; I could quite see that. Now I understood the frustration of the administrator I'd talked to at Head Office. Describing a fragment of a Restoration roundelay, for example, as being *two inches down in the third pile to the right on the small mahogany table in the far room* would be less than ideal as far as information retrieval went.

'It's magnificent,' I said, not needing to fake the reverence in my voice. 'I'll try not to cause too much upheaval, but if we are going to turn it into a working research facility, I'm afraid it will need a fair bit of reorganising.'

Leonard gave an irritable sigh and gestured crossly to a bookcase bay with a window looking out onto Almoner's Place. I could see a shiny new laptop and printer on the desk, presumably for me. Through the narrow window, just as it did next door, the cathedral loomed startlingly close above the roofline of the High Street.

'Thank you,' I said. 'That looks perfect.' I took a chance and smiled at him. 'But what I'd really love is for you to show me around before I start work properly. If you only knew how many times I've tracked down the only known copy of something, only to find it belongs to you . . . '

My new boss glared at me, but I sensed he was pleased. 'Very well. In the first room, we have . . . '

★ ★ ★

A couple of hours later, I was dazed
and elated and full of utter wonder that
I had landed a job amongst such
treasures. Not that the task would be
easy. The collection was an immense,
glorious shambles. It was a good thing I
had patience, logic, tenacity, and an
extendable contract.

I located the staff kitchen downstairs,
made two mugs of tea and brought
them back up, being very careful not to
put mine anywhere near any precious
manuscripts. 'I enjoyed the music you
were playing last night,' I said, handing
Leonard his mug. 'Lovely voices. Which
recording was it?'

Leonard's eyebrows rose austerely.
'Playing? Heaven forbid. My interest is
in the written work. I prefer to listen to
the score in my head, unsullied by
modern interpretations.'

I stared. 'But I heard Gregorian

39

plainsong. It must have been you.'

'It most certainly was not. I was upstairs studying and comparing Italian ballads. One cannot do that distracted by external influences.' Now he was looking offended.

'Sorry,' I said, and gave him my best rueful smile. 'I was obviously more tired than I realised. I had the Dorian Singers on my iPod coming up on the train. They must have worked their way into my head.'

He hrmphed and went down to the far end of the room. I started up my new computer. Despite my words to Leonard, I knew what I'd heard: children's voices in trained harmony, not an echo of memory from a train journey several hours before.

I glanced through the window. The cathedral filled the panes, but it wasn't anything like near enough to hear the sound of the choir. If the singing hadn't been coming through the wall from Leonard's flat, where *had* it been coming from?

3

The mystery of the singing continued to hover at the edge of my mind as I worked. Gregorian plainsong wasn't the sort of thing you imagined. If Leonard said it hadn't been him playing a CD, I couldn't think where the music had come from. Outside, maybe? The windows weren't soundproof for all they fitted snugly. I think I'd have noticed a choir standing on the pavement, though, especially at midnight. Nor would it have been a car radio for that length of time, because there wasn't room in Almoner's Place to park.

The other explanation was that Dr Leonard Smith was not being straight with me. I had no idea why he should deny listening to the music he filled his life with, but it seemed to me (admittedly on very new acquaintance) that he was not a happy man. Not all the time, anyway. When he was walking around the library explaining about the collection, getting out a pamphlet to share an anecdote about its history or pulling down a manuscript to tell me where he had come by it, the grey hair circling his tonsure fluffed up and he grew filled-out and animated. Then he'd absently stroke a sheet of vellum, tracing out the notes inked on it centuries ago . . . and his hand would tremble and he'd snatch it away as if angry that I might have seen.

I'd met a lot of academics over the years, but none quite like Leonard. There were the know-everythings, who did nothing but talk and applaud their own cleverness and who expected constant admiration from their acolytes. There were also genuine teachers who knew their subject and enjoyed passing their knowledge on, getting satisfaction out of making you think and coaxing your best efforts out of you. But Leonard wasn't either of these types.

He knew his material, and he'd written any number of definitive papers on the development of early music and its gradual spread across Europe, but as I observed him now, I came to realise it was almost as if he wrote these treatises for his own benefit. He didn't want to teach or inform; he simply wanted to set the record straight. He wanted it *right*. He was in love with the facts, and with reasoned deduction.

'You previously worked for Jonathan Ambergris,' he said suddenly.

For a moment my heart gave a painful lurch. I forced myself to look up casually. 'Yes, that's right. I prepared the fact sheets on sales items for the firm and maintained the database.'

Leonard tapped his fingers on a shelf. 'Did you examine the Italian psalter he acquired in the Rome sale in January?'

I thought back. 'Only briefly. It went straight out to a client, so I didn't have time to look at it in any depth.'

'He paid too much for it, which is

why I dropped out.'

'The client was very keen,' I said. Also important, which was presumably why Jon had reduced his profit margin on that deal.

'Pity you didn't see it. Not that I believe it to be significantly different to the one here, also penned at the same monastery, but confirmation would have been useful.'

I smiled to myself and continued to rough out my ideas for cataloguing the collection. I was coming to the inescapable conclusion that the only workable way was to start at one end of one room and simply work steadily through, left to right, top to bottom, adding notes on everything I could think of as I went. This could take years.

* * *

On the grounds that eating with the house team would be friendlier than nipping home, and that I could probably do with the company, I'd brought a sandwich with me for lunch, intending to wash it down with a mug of tea in the staff kitchen. I got there to find the teapot full and the builders very ready to squeeze up to make room for me at the table.

'The new housing for the collection,' I said to Ewan. 'Where's it going to be? What's it going to be like?'

Ewan rolled his eyes and the carpenters groaned. 'It's going to be everywhere we can fit a shelf. And as for what it's going to be like — well, you tell me,' he said. 'The foundation would like glass-fronted cases with security locks and temperature controls, but it's not the most accessible of solutions.'

I winced. 'Leonard's going to hate that.'

'Well, now would be the time to change the design,' said Ewan blandly. 'That's if you can get him to talk about what he might like instead. I'm happy to make alterations, provided that the security aspect is addressed, but I can't do anything without a clear directive. In the absence of Leonard doing the directing, I have to follow the Newrigg specifications.'

'I'll have a word with him,' I said.

He raised his eyebrows. 'I wish you better luck than I had.'

The trouble was, I realised as I watched Leonard move around his jumbled scholar's paradise during the afternoon, he loved his library. Each book, each sheet of music, all the individually crafted staves and notes — they were as children to him. He wouldn't want to see them locked away behind glass. Was that why he was unhappy — because he'd given his beloved possessions over to the Newrigg Foundation for their own good, and was finding it hard to come to terms with?

Confirmation came in a roundabout way the next day. An email had been forwarded to me by my particular director at Newrigg. It contained a series of requests from a researcher who wanted to examine a particular text. Each time it had been requested, Leonard had replied that it was unavailable at present. This was very strange, because if I turned my head I could look directly at the folio in question, nestled between two others in the bookcase beside me.

I rubbed my nose irresolutely. Presumably the email had been sent to me because the director's secretary was getting no joy from Leonard. I suspected I would be dealing with all such requests from now on. That was fine by me — in fact, I thought it a very good idea — but handling them would be tricky if Leonard wasn't cooperating.

I waited for him to make one of his regular forays into my part of the room. He did this all over the library — selecting a particular book or a certain paper, then bearing them off to his long refectory-style table at the far end.

'What'll happen when someone asks

to study a book?' I said, leaning back and stretching as if I had been sitting too long. 'Is there going to be a secure reading room downstairs?'

Out of the corner of my eye, I saw Leonard contract. His fingers tightened on the worn board cover in his hand and he really did seem to shrink inside his skin. A grey frost touched his face. 'We don't need to think about that yet. There's plenty of time.' There was an air of finality in his voice.

So he *had* been stalling. I was seized by a sharp burst of compassion. He'd spent a lifetime and all his money on these books and manuscripts. Naturally he didn't want them mishandled, much less go out into the world on a mere promise that they would be returned. However, the Newrigg Foundation's position had been made abundantly clear. From the tone of that email, if Leonard didn't start complying with requests, he could find himself ousted for good. I'd known him for a very short space of time in person, but I'd known of him and revered him for years. I had to do something.

'It's *exactly* the right time to start thinking about it,' I said, jumping up, all bright-eyed and conspiratorial. 'If nothing has been specified yet, that's fantastic! It'll be contingency planning, don't you see? You get to set your own parameters and conditions for the researchers before it's done for you. Oh, this is too good an opportunity to miss. I think we need to organise a reading room with Ewan Matlock as soon as possible. He's the site manager for the house, so he must have the authority to okay the plans. If we design every last detail ourselves and show the situation will be viable, then by the time researchers start making requests of the library, your ideal procedure will be in place. The Newrigg Foundation would have to make a very strong case for changing an existing system that's already been proved to work well. Shall I ask Ewan if he can make a meeting tomorrow? There's no time to lose if we want to take the wind out of the foundation's sails.'

Leonard stirred. 'My terms . . . ' he murmured. I saw the same spark come back into his eyes that had been there yesterday when he'd been telling me about routing a competitor by discovering that the auction day for an obscure treatise on Léonin and Pérotin had been moved forward.

'Exactly,' I said, piling on the enthusiasm. 'Your terms. Your rules. The first thing to do is to consider all the different places where you've studied documents. Which were the best and which were the worst? Use your experience of them to decide what you want or don't want here. It's not for me to say, but it seems to me that if you make the reading room comfortable — not here in your library, I'd suggest, because these are the last rooms the builders will be dealing with, and we want something ready as soon as possible — with large tables and a good light, then it'll be a nice atmosphere for researchers, and no one will be able to make a case for taking any books off the premises. Obviously there'll be security cameras and a guard on the door, and I'll devise a booking-out system; but no time limit, don't you think? I always get so mad when I'm told the two hours or whatever is up.'

'No gloves,' said Leonard suddenly. 'Parchment and vellum are living pages. They are made for human skin, not abrasive cotton gloves.'

Yes! He'd made a suggestion of his own and, crucially, he hadn't refuted the idea of a designated reading room. I could have cheered from the rafters. I made a show of opening a new file on my laptop and typing it in. 'What else?' I asked, my fingers poised above the keyboard. 'Only pencils to be used in the reading room as usual? Laptops allowed, do you think? It's quicker for taking notes, so the researchers will be through sooner.'

'Yes, that's good, and . . . '

With every word he grew more alert. I typed his thoughts as he voiced them. By the time we'd compiled a first draft, he'd lost that head-in-the-sand, blanking-out look. I left him having a nice spirited argument with a fellow enthusiast over the phone about the later compositions of Henry Purcell while I slipped downstairs to find Ewan.

'A reading room?' Ewan scrubbed a hand through his dark hair (incidentally revealing why it always looked messy) as thoughts chased across his face. 'No,' he said in a considering voice. 'No, there's nothing on the plans about a reading room. Possibly Newrigg were envisioning people sitting at small tables to study all over the house. A monitored reading room is a terrific idea. I've been worried about Leonard's reaction to having security guards camped in his library all day while researchers wander around at will. I'll have a think and get something ready for tomorrow.' He smiled at me. 'You're all right, you know. Well done.'

I was startled by the praise. It wasn't personal. He meant I was being good for Leonard. I was also intrigued that he'd seen that — and that he approved.

★   ★   ★

My belongings turned up mid-afternoon. I chuckled gleefully as I ran down the stairs to let the delivery men into No. 4. Living in a company-flat environment was all very well, but I wanted to meld my personality with that of the house. My rental agreement was for a year with the option to renew, and I wanted to feel truly at home here. We stacked everything in the shop area for speed, then as soon as I finished work, I raced back and gloated. With silent apologies to my mother and her fixed belief in fresh produce made into home-cooked meals, I put a ready meal in the microwave and undid the first carton.

My mobile rang. I looked up,

expecting the sound to be the shop door. I barely had time to wonder why I should think that when I realised it was the phone. Flustered, and wanting to get back to my unpacking, I answered without looking at the display.

'Hi, Clare.'

My stomach swooped badly. It was Jonathan. He'd stopped off at the Queen's Arms after work, by the background sounds. And he was calling me because that was what he did when I wasn't also stopping off with him for an illicit twenty minutes on his way home.

'Hi, Jon,' I said cautiously. 'How are you?'

'Lonely. Feeling like a fool.'

I had to ward against the twisting of my heart. 'There are so many things I could say to that, but we've said them already. Why are you calling? We agreed not to. I'm making a fresh start, Jon.'

'I know, darling, but I wanted to know how you are. I wanted to be sure you'd got there all right. I care for you.'

Of course he did. But he also cared for his wife, his children, his job, and his standing in the community. To my shame, I found I had tears on my cheeks. 'I care for me too,' I said. 'That's why I came away. I need my own life, Jonathan, I told you. I can't live a half-existence any more. I deserve better. Marianne deserves better.'

'I know, my dear. I wish . . . I just wanted to check you were all right. How's the new job? What's the set-up like? Do you have much to do with Leonard Smith?'

A month ago I would have told him everything. Even now, the impulse to do so trembled on my tongue. 'It's fine. Interesting. It's going to keep me very busy. Jon, I think you should ring off. This isn't a good idea.'

'I'd like to call now and again to make sure you're okay. If you don't mind?'

I let the words lie for a moment. His voice was so soft, so loving, so Jonathan. 'I think I do mind,' I said slowly. 'It's over. Just picture me happy and I'll picture you content.'

'I miss you, Clare.'

I had everything clenched now. I would not let him hear the tears in my voice. 'You've no reason to,' I said. 'You've got everything you need.'

'I haven't got you. I miss talking to you. Marianne is too busy spending a fortune redecorating the nursery to spend time just talking.'

'That's not my fault, Jon. Redecorate the nursery with her.'

'I could come and see you. It wouldn't be difficult to make a diversion when I'm at an auction or meeting a client out that way.'

'No,' I said. 'You're not being fair. Just leave me alone. Please.'

'I'll still think of you.' There was a wealth of sadness in his tone. I recognised it as a subtle attempt at manipulation and braced myself against it.

'Look after yourself, Jonathan,' I said. 'Goodbye.'

I fumbled the phone off, about to have a good howl. In the kitchen, the microwave beeped insistently. I gave a mighty sniff, blew my nose and went to get out my food. So much for my brave resolutions, if just the sound of Jon's voice could set me off. I was never going to be able to cope with this.

As I was sliding the microwaved meal onto a plate, I heard a soft sound from the shop. I hurried back out and saw a couple of my cushions lying on the floor. There was a distinctly guilty feel to the air.

'That crate may be full,' I said aloud, 'but cushions do not spontaneously burst out of crates for no reason. Is this like the sheets, but in reverse?' I carried an armload of the cushions upstairs and strewed the bright summery colours around the neutral living room.

'That's better!' I said. 'More home, less executive rest area.' And felt, with a prickling of my spine, a trace of curiosity in the room.

I told myself I was imagining things. I

sat down to eat my beef dinner for one, studying the long wall opposite, trying to think what it might need by way of decoration. Not a mirror. Not a modern print. Something rich, something colourful, something like a . . .

Tapestry.

The word dropped into my head out of nowhere. 'Tapestry?' I repeated aloud before I could stop myself.

A picture appeared in my mind, of a room the full length of this floor — this room, in fact, before it had been partitioned — with sunlight streaming across cushioned benches and a curtained bed at the far end. A tapestry hung on the wall, dense with detail, rich with red and blue. Before the image of the room disappeared, I saw women sewing, children playing on the floor, a boy whittling on the window seat, a man tending the fire . . .

I sat utterly still. My fork clattered onto my plate. Had I really seen that? After a minute when nothing else happened, I looked at my meal, decided

I didn't want it after all, then heard my mother's voice in my head saying I was too thin and didn't I know how many starving people there were in the world who could live on that plateful for a week.

'What was all that about?' I said, eating again.

There was . . . not exactly silence; more an absence of anyone answering.

I am not going mad.

I said it again out loud: 'I am not going mad.'

Instead of panicking, I analysed possible explanations. I had an affinity with this house. I'd instinctively known where everything was as soon as I'd walked in, hadn't I? Seeing a snapshot of the past would just be one more instance of it. All the same, there *was* someone here. Feeling a little self-conscious, I cleared my throat.

'When are you from?' I asked into the silence. 'What era?'

This time I sensed a shrug, as if whatever the presence was, it had no real concept of time.

'Who is on the throne?'

Elizabeth.

I knew, absolutely knew, that they didn't mean Elizabeth Windsor. I took a very deep breath. 'Was that you singing the other night? I really liked it.'

Again a shrug, a ripple in the air. But this one was matter-of-fact, an 'I expect so.' And then the presence was gone. It was so gone that I knew I hadn't imagined it being there before.

I finished the rest of my meal without tasting it. I was still absorbing the . . . I suppose I'd have to call it an exchange. If anything, I was relieved at it rather than alarmed. Whoever it was that flitted in and out of this house, they were young and benign. And the house still felt like mine. It had also done me a favour, I realised later. It had succeeded in pushing Jonathan to the very edge of my mind. Which was where he could stay.

I unpacked the rest of my belongings: my books, my music, my crockery, my pots and pans. The cathedral dominated the windows as I went to and fro between the rooms, up and down between the floors. I glanced at it speculatively. Was that where my ethereal visitors were from? It had to be, surely. The singing I'd heard on my first night here had been sacred rather than secular, and I had a feeling it had been on the edge of my hearing since then as well. I still didn't understand quite how I'd heard it, but I was fairly sure I was right.

It was strange how the cathedral looked so near, even though it wasn't. Some trick of the design, perhaps, because everything about it was larger and heavier and taller than the buildings surrounding it. My eyes ranged over the profusion of narrow windows and stone curlicues. Dad had always seen busman's holiday tours as a useful way to network, to become known in the church hierarchy. Every summer for years had been spent familiarising ourselves with church buildings and church ministries all over the country. Ely was one of the few cathedrals we'd missed. It was odd, not knowing it.

Well, I decided, even if that horrible, shiver-inducing cold spot on the green *was* something to do with why I'd screamed the place down, I wasn't eight years old anymore, and no cathedral was going to get the better of me. I'd go and introduce myself tomorrow lunchtime. Perhaps I'd find out more about my mysterious singers.

4

Up close, the Cathedral Church of the Holy and Undivided Trinity at Ely took my breath away. It surged in a welter of massive, gothic, carved blond stone to tower over the town. Standing across the road, I found it impossible to take in the whole structure. It was just so enormous, so out of scale with the surroundings. I had to tilt my head right back in order to look at the very top of the tower. Even for someone brought up with churches like I had been, the nine-hundred-year-old building was awe-inspiring. It was so peculiar not knowing it. Maybe once I was inside, this vague unresolved feeling would leave me.

As I crossed the main road, my gaze skidded sideways to the triangle of grass in front of the Bishop's Palace where I'd stepped into that moment of terror and stuck fast. That too would have to be faced, but not right now. I preferred my problems one at a time. I turned my back on the green, repeating to myself that avoiding it wasn't cowardice. For one thing, I had work to get back to this afternoon, and for another, seeing what the cathedral had for me in the way of rogue singers was quite enough for today.

Ely cathedral was as vast inside as it was outside. You could have fitted a small village in here and still had room to pasture the cows. I realised as soon as I walked in through the west door that I wouldn't have time for the full cathedral tour; that could wait for the weekend. Instead I paid my admission fee and sat in the nave for a few minutes, looking up at the immense arched roof and imagining how much music it would take to fill it.

Before I'd come to Ely, I'd read a little about its history. For centuries, the surrounding fenland had been marsh and water. The principal trade had been by river with King's Lynn. There were few roads. Wool merchants had needed fen guides to bring their wares safely from Norwich and Bury St Edmunds. The monastery, as it was then, had grown rich in isolation, islanded on its bed of raised clay with its cluster of nearby streets to provide services for the monks. The town is still called the Isle of Ely even though Thomas Cromwell facilitated the draining of the fens when he inherited land here during the seventeenth century, so now there are houses and roads spreading out from the centre.

I explored, getting the feel of the building. It was difficult with something so large. Time moved at a different rate here. When I rested my hand on a pillar, I sensed a lofty calm. There had been unpleasantness, but it had been long ago. The cathedral looked after the town, and was succoured by it; neither would have existed without the other. The building knew it was venerated. That was all it needed.

In the shop I bought proper histories of Ely and the cathedral, and collected a fistful of leaflets on the locality. I also gathered up my resolution and with a tiny, diffident thrill asked about local choirs. It felt strange, after five years of structuring my time around stolen moments with Jon, to be clumsily weaving together the threads of a life just for me. I'd always sung, but I'd let my choir membership in London lapse because practice was on Thursday nights, which was the only evening Jonathan could get away. If his phone call yesterday had taught me anything at all, it was that I had to start thinking of myself again. Getting out, meeting people and doing something I loved, like singing in harmony, would be a good first step. Yes, I said to the information desk receptionist as she fished out choir leaflets for me, I could do any evening, any weekend.

The loneliness, I told myself, would go.

It wasn't until I'd settled down to

my indexing again in the quiet of the Newrigg Foundation library, having been only slightly distracted by the market stalls in the High Street on the way back, that I realised I was no further on as far as my own small conundrum was concerned. The cathedral might fill every window I walked past, but it no longer coloured the life of the town as it had in the days when ninety percent of the population depended on it for their daily bread. I'd been taking its authority for granted, quite why I didn't know, but it hadn't told me anything new. When I'd walked around inside, it hadn't held any familiar echoes. In short, it hadn't affected me at all. I felt surprise run right through me as I worked out what this meant. It meant that although I was still interested in the history of the cathedral for its own sake, my personal puzzle was centred elsewhere.

That elsewhere, I suspected, was No. 4 Almoner's Place.

* ★ ★ ★

'Why did you choose to live in Ely and start the collection here?' I asked Leonard when we stopped for tea that afternoon. 'Was it because of the cathedral?'

He looked mildly bewildered. 'I've always been here,' he said, as if I should have known such an obvious thing. He smoothed down his ring of grey hair. 'This is my family house. When I was young, we lived in one part of it and my paternal grandparents lived in the section that would have originally been No. 3, though the rooms were all connected even then. I believe at one stage the house was used as a school.'

I gave a happy wriggle. 'I love learning about how buildings develop. Sorry, I didn't mean to be nosy. I just wondered, being so close to the cathedral.'

Leonard glanced through the window to where the building in question loomed over the rooftops. 'The cathedral may well be where my interest in early music came from. My parents used to say I sang plainsong before I could talk.'

I had a sudden difficulty in keeping a straight face, picturing an elderly, irascible baby warbling motets and madrigals in his cradle instead of nursery rhymes. 'How wonderful,' I managed. 'Were you a boy chorister?'

A wintry smile passed across his face. 'Yes, indeed. Then my voice broke and I studied the music instead of singing it. I wanted to *know*. I wanted to know its origins, how it had developed. When it had turned into different parts for different voices. When the underlying drone was lost. I wanted to trace the spread of it.' He looked reflectively around the library. 'It's possible I became a little obsessed.'

It was in that moment I fell completely in love with Leonard. 'It's a magnificent achievement,' I said. 'Has your family always lived here then?

How far back can you trace?'

'Several generations.' He waved towards the furthest of the interconnecting rooms. 'In the chest in the corner are old maps of Ely describing the house, how it used to be three dwellings and so on. I found them when I was looking for the deeds for the Newrigg Foundation.'

I winced. Signing away his family home couldn't have been easy even if he had no one to pass it on to in his turn. 'Do you retain any rights?' I asked sympathetically.

I'd misjudged him. He gave that faint smile again. 'I wasn't quite born yesterday, Clare.'

I took the empty mugs downstairs, where I found Ewan washing up after the building team's break. 'You're very domesticated,' I said in surprise. In my experience, workmen, academics and high-flying arts dealers alike all tended to leave dirty crockery for the cleaning fairies.

'The perils of having a doctor for a

father,' said Ewan cheerfully. 'Germs never stood a chance in our house.' He added my mugs to the suds-filled bowl and handed me a tea towel. 'I've incorporated your reading room into the downstairs plans. Is Leonard busy? I'd like to run through it with him.'

'He'd be delighted,' I said firmly.

Ewan cocked an eyebrow at me. 'You've fallen for him, haven't you?'

I flapped the tea towel at him. 'And you haven't? Ewan, Leonard is safe here, isn't he? The Newrigg Foundation can't turn him out?'

Ewan grinned reassuringly. 'Tenant for life. We're not even allowed to interfere with his flat unless he asks.'

'That's good,' I said with relief.

'But they could still shift the collection itself if he doesn't play ball.'

I nodded. I'd expected that. I'd just have to teach Leonard the rules of the game.

There was a shout from the front of the house. 'Delivery next door,' called one of the men.

I exchanged a look with Ewan. 'I've got all my stuff. I'm not expecting anything more,' I said, hurrying to see what it was.

The delivery man was already heading this way, carrying a large box. 'Name of Somerset?' he asked.

'Yes, that's me.'

'Sign here, then.'

I saw the logo of a florist on the side of the box and smiled. It must be Mum, sending me a happy-new-house arrangement. 'Flowers from my mother,' I said, peering in at the top. 'I'll just nip upstairs for my keys and take them next door, then we can tackle Leonard. Where are you thinking of for the reading room?'

'The room to the right of the front door here. It'll open straight off the enlarged entrance hall, so people can go straight into it and it reduces the need for visitors to wander all over the place.' Ewan steered me towards it. 'Is it about the right size, do you think? It was two smaller rooms originally, as you can see, but we can widen the connecting arch quite safely and put mirrors at the far end so people can't hide in any blind spots and doodle on the pages.' He said this last with a faint grin.

'Or even slice them out,' I said grimly. 'I've known that happen. Some dealers aren't interested in the folios as unique works; they just want to turn the illustrated pages into authentic framed gifts for the person who has everything. Vandals.'

Ewan made a note on his pad. '*Big* mirrors,' he emphasised. His voice was grave, but the corners of his mouth twitched. I fixed him with a look. I couldn't work out whether he was teasing or humouring me.

* * *

After work, I extracted the floral arrangement from its box. It was a bouquet of reds, oranges, and yellows. Summer colours. Beautiful, I thought happily, until I saw three tightly budded dark red roses nestled in the centre. I looked at them with misgiving.

Hand-tied for a perfect display! read the label. It then added bossily, *Do not rearrange, but you may remove the outer cellophane to facilitate the introduction of your arrangement into a vase.*

Big of them, I thought, fetching a vase. Was there a flower food sachet? Yes, there was. I pulled it out and dislodged a small card. I read it.

From all at Jonathan Ambergris Fine Art & Music, with best wishes for your new career. We will miss you.

The card fell from my fingers. I'd known as soon as I'd seen those roses. Not my mother. Jonathan. Every careless bunch of flowers he'd ever given me had had three dark red roses included. His secret signature, he'd told me with a smile. Three roses. Three little words.

I put the bouquet in water anyway, because I couldn't bear the waste of throwing the flowers away after all the effort that had been put into growing and arranging them, but I left the vase at the far end of the shop counter instead of taking it upstairs to the living room as I would have done had the gift been from Mum.

'It's not your fault you were given to me by an idiot,' I said to it. 'Which part of *It's over, Jonathan* did he not understand, do you suppose?' All the same, those three roses had taken the shine off my mood. I went upstairs to change into cooler clothes.

Something I'd encountered during the day was nagging at me, but I couldn't pin it down. Something at the cathedral? Something at work? I didn't know. It sat at the back of my mind, annoyingly just out of prodding range. The best thing to do in those circumstances, I'd always found, was to think of something else. Preferably something other than Jon not leaving me alone.

I changed into a sleeveless top and leaned my arms on my bedroom windowsill, breathing in the evening air. Outside, it was both busy and peaceful at the same time. The sounds of market traders packing up in the next street was clearly audible: clanking poles, lorry engines revving, stall-holders shouting to one another. But overlaid above that, causing a sudden tingle of awareness to run up my spine, was church singing — polyphonic parts this time; young, pure voices.

I didn't move a muscle. I stayed exactly where I was and concentrated on the lovely soaring music. It *could* be coming from the cathedral, I thought — the sound quality was about right — but I'd have bet large sums of money that were I to shut the window, I'd hear it still. It seemed to me that the singing floated above the sounds of the outdoor market like a veil, unimpeded by anything, not sharing the same space but on a different plane altogether. The liquid notes hung in the air in the same way that a tracing-paper drawing has no effect on the image beneath it on the real page.

Had they once lived in this house, the choirboys? And had they practised so often that their voices existed outside of time? I remembered what Leonard had said about singing plainsong before he could talk. I wondered whether he had heard these same canticles, perhaps, as he lay in his cradle next door, and been subliminally affected by the purity of the notes for the rest of his life.

How could I find out about the cathedral choir in historic times? Were there records? As I listened to voices as ageless as any I'd heard in Paris and Florence and Ghent, and stared at the hotchpotch of roofs behind Almoner's Place framing unlovely yards and impossibly parked cars, my mind's eye did another flick. I drew in a sharp breath as I worked out what I was seeing.

Gone were the present-day buildings below my window. Instead there was a much longer yard attached to the house, with a dog tied up and hens scratching in the dirt. Beyond the yard there was an area of green containing two goats and a cow, with a small girl watching them. There were trees, bushes, and a scratched-out tillage with onions and plants I didn't recognise. Wooden hurdles divided my green patch from next door's similar set-up, and again from the one beyond that. At the far end of the row, the yard held a fat pig in a small sty and a pond with ducks.

A noise of sawing floated up to me. Someone was hammering as well, and there was the chink of a chisel. Movement caught my eye. An old woman sat in the sunshine on my side of the yard, carding wool. Just for a moment she looked up, blue eyes piercing mine; then her attention shifted as two neatly dressed young women approached her from the house. *Supplicants*, I thought, but didn't know why.

And then the picture flicked off. I wanted to cry out with loss, to call for it to come back, but it had provided the answer to my niggle. Leonard's maps — I wanted to examine them. 1–3 Almoner's Place had been in his family for generations, even if originally it hadn't been all one dwelling. The old drawings of the house that he'd mentioned might hold clues to the history of No. 4 as well. There had to be a reason I was getting all these flashbacks of my house. At the very least, the plans could give me a starting point for finding out why.

The vision wasn't coming back. As I straightened up, I realised I had another possible line of research, albeit an unconventional one. While I'd been watching the garden — attached, as it were, to the past — the singing had definitely strengthened in that upper plane. I was certain now that the music belonged to this house. Jerking into action, I ran downstairs and upended the bag of history books I'd bought at the cathedral. The semi-rural garden scene, my tapestry-hung living room, the singing . . . everything came together to guide my hurtling thoughts. Riffling through the book on the cathedral, I came to the passage I'd seen briefly at lunchtime.

'In 1568 Queen Elizabeth the First ordered that there should be one master of the choristers and eight singing boys,' I read aloud.

The singing stopped in mid-bar. The air about me rippled and my senses tingled.

'You *are* the singing boys from the cathedral?' I said.

Assent came through the air.

Oh my goodness, I was right. This was crazy. I wanted to scream and laugh at the same time. I wanted to clutch at my hair and hug myself. There were ghosts in my house and I was *communicating* with them. I didn't think it was all eight of the boys mentioned in the book; they had all been there during the singing, I was sure, but I only got the feeling of there being two or three present now.

Just how did one talk to ghosts? 'What are your names?' I asked helplessly.

Thomas.

Robert.

I'd been right — just two. It was making me feel very odd that I'd been able to tell. What did it mean? Why were they here?

I was aware of amusement as they picked up my thoughts. There was a silent piling-up of feather-laughter in the air. They let me know they were here because they lived here, of course. Thomas was the son of the house. Robert, his friend, lodged with them to be near for the services and the teaching. Along with that intelligence came a rush of images — of sheep in fields, fleeces washed in a stream, hides pegged out in the running water. I couldn't swear to it, but I was left with the impression that Robert's family might be tanners.

'Why can I hear you?' I asked aloud.

A shrug as they faded out, following

the rest of the choir over towards the cathedral. *You have the gift.*

It was accompanied by a flash of the old woman I'd seen in the sixteenth-century garden.

5

I ground my teeth in frustration. So near to getting answers, and then my ghostly singing boys were gone, leaving me with a scrap of knowledge and yet more questions. What did they mean by saying I had 'the gift'? Who was the woman in the garden? Why was she significant?

This was too enormous for me to deal with by myself. I needed another person to share my thoughts with. Preferably someone who wouldn't have me committed. That was easy, then. I phoned my mother.

'Clare, how lovely. Hello, darling, how are you? Are you eating properly yet? I'm getting an order sent down to you from my butcher here. I put to ring next door if there was no answer. Is that okay?'

'Yes, but — '

'Good. How's the job?'

'The job is absolute heaven. It's going to take me at least a year, probably more.' I paused, trying to frame my next sentence.

'But . . . ?' prompted my mother.

'But . . . I think my house is haunted,' I said baldly. I paced back and forth, looking out of the window as if half-expecting the garden to reappear.

'Properly haunted, Clare? Or just one of your little friends again?'

I nearly dropped the phone. That was the last reply I'd expected. 'Little friends? What are you talking about? I don't have any little friends.'

'You used to have, dear, don't you remember? When we were living in that dreadful draughty place in Yorkshire, I often used to hear you talking to no one. You said they were just some friends. Afterwards, we found they once lived there. You had the right names and everything.'

I sat down abruptly, sweat sheeting over me. I *did* remember, but up until

84

this moment I had completely blanked it out and forgotten. 'Mum, I was six years old when we lived in Yorkshire.'

She was unperturbed. 'Are these ghosts the same?'

I thought back, shaken, to that half-remembered time when I had played, unconcerned, with non-corporeal children in the old nursery wing of a monstrosity of a Victorian rectory. 'Yes.'

'There you are, then, darling. There's nothing to be worried about. You can always track them down if you want to.'

Track them down. Just like that. 'Aren't you even a *little* bit concerned about me?' I asked.

'Of course I am, dear. But if you thought your ghosts weren't benign, you'd have called your father, not me. Now then, what are the shops like? Have you bought anything nice?'

I gave a reluctant laugh. 'Mum, sometimes you don't sound like a clergy wife at all.'

She sighed comfortably. 'I know. It's such a trial to your father.'

* * *

'Could I look at those plans you mentioned?' I asked Leonard the next day. 'Do they show details of my house as well as yours? I'm interested in its history. Ewan says it used to be a shop.'

Leonard snorted. 'A shop of sorts. It sold insurance most recently. When I was young it was a gentleman's outfitter. You are welcome to look through the plans. I think you'll like them. They're rather interesting, show-ing the way the external area has changed over time.'

He was suspiciously eager for me to avail myself. I knew what he was thinking — that if I was studying the history of Almoner's Place, it would be that much longer before the database was ready and he had to allow strangers in to do their research using *his* books.

'Thanks,' I said. 'I'll get the maps out during my break.' Leonard gave an irritable sigh. I let my hair hang forward to hide my grin.

Unfortunately, when the time came, he couldn't find the key to the chest, so I was sent down to ask Ewan Matlock for advice on breaking and entering. I located him amidst a plethora of building supplies in the disused kitchen from No. 3.

'It's a warren, this place, isn't it?' I said. 'I'm getting the hang of it though.'

'I find it helps me picture where pipes and drains might be if I think of it as three separate houses,' Ewan said absently, an intent expression on his face as he studied a built-in cupboard to one side of the deep brick fireplace.

'I've been doing that since Leonard told me his grandparents lived in this end when he was a boy,' I confessed. 'Why are you looking puzzled? Have you got problems?'

'The proportions don't match.' He stared into the open cupboard, then at the fireplace. 'I think there's a false end to this cupboard. Are you busy? Can you hold the end of the tape measure for a moment so I can check?'

'Sure,' I said.

He began to shift boxes of fittings until he'd cleared a narrow aisle down the centre of the cupboard.

'Do you want me to squeeze in?' I asked. 'I'm thinner than you.'

'That would be helpful, if you don't mind.'

We swapped places. I edged in, holding the end of the tape measure in front of me. I accidentally stubbed my toe on one of the boxes and put a hand on the wall to steady myself — and instantly got a blast of fear, right into my soul. I screamed.

'What's the matter? What have you done?' Ewan's voice was shockingly close, pulling me out of the sweating nothingness even as he physically closed his hand around my wrist.

'I don't . . . ' I croaked. I cleared my throat and tried again. 'I don't think you should . . . that is, I think you should leave the back of the cupboard where it is.'

The brick walls inside the cupboard

had been painted white. With the door wide open, it gave enough reflected light for me to see Ewan's face, still holding my wrist and looking at me in concern. 'Meaning what?' he asked. 'Take your time.' And to one of the carpenters who'd heard me scream and was running into the kitchen to investigate: 'It's okay, Hamid. Clare was helping me measure this cupboard and she tripped. She's fine.'

Ewan was taking me seriously, which meant he believed I could sense something here. Just that one fact gave me the confidence to believe in it myself. I closed my eyes and tried to sort out the sensations I was getting. 'There's a lot of fear,' I said, bracing myself against it. 'But there's sadness too. Why would that be? Fear and sorrow mixed together. That doesn't make sense.'

I wrinkled my brow, groping after a thread of something else. Underlying the emotions was a faint presence that I almost recognised. That scared me. I didn't want to know anyone who was feeling this heartsick. I shook my head angrily and barricaded it out.

Ewan kept that sturdy, comforting hold on my arm. 'Is there a body walled up there? Can you tell?'

I gasped and stared at him in horror. I hadn't even thought of bodies. But I suppose with him specialising in old buildings, it was something he might have come across before. How ghastly for him. 'I don't think so,' I said. I was feeling really ill now. I just wanted to leave this room forever.

His voice gentled. 'Concentrate, Clare. Is it old sadness? Is it despair?'

He was thinking it might be a priest hole. I'd wondered that. 'I can't really date it. It's just there, imprinted in this spot. Fear and sorrow, and maybe a sense of purpose. I'm not getting pain, or hunger or thirst, so I don't think there can be a skeleton. I'm sorry I screamed.'

'I think a scream is natural under the circumstances,' he said dryly. He let go of my arm, then studied the smooth surface of the thickly painted bricks at the far end, shining a pocket torch around the edges. 'That's some talent you have. No clue as to how we might access the space, I suppose?'

I ran my hand over the wall and noticed Ewan's eyes flick neutrally to it. Along with the same mixture of emotions, I got a sense of having to stoop. That was all. I told him so.

'Okay, I'll put a couple of the lads onto it while I have my meeting with the surveyor,' said Ewan. 'I'm sorry I let you in for that. It wasn't my intention.'

'It wasn't my expectation,' I replied, still unnerved.

'And I made it worse by asking.'

'No,' I said slowly. 'No, I think you made it better. If I hadn't carried on, I'd have been left with the shock of that first impression. As it was, you made me think it through and apply logic to it. It turned it into an analytical problem, rather than a purely emotional experience.'

He scrubbed his hair doubtfully. 'If you say so. Have you got anything to give you a quick energy boost? Biscuits? Chocolate?' At my look of incomprehension he rolled his eyes and left the room, returning with two chocolate flapjacks. 'Eat, don't argue.'

'You have flapjacks! Have you been talking to my mother? She's convinced I need feeding up.'

'No, they were from a fête at Mum's school. We were all under instructions to buy something. Nice, aren't they?'

I nodded, my mouth full of sticky oats and golden syrup. 'Why were you looking for me, by the way?'

'Oh, I'd forgotten.' He was right, I did feel better now. I licked my fingers and explained about Leonard's chest.

'A pair of long-nose pliers will probably do the trick, though we'll have to be careful. Let's have a look.' With a little manipulation, the chest did indeed open, though not without some slight damage to the lock and surrounding wood, which made me flinch.

The contents were enough to distract me from any number of priest holes. As Leonard had said, the maps were fascinating. There were several of Almoner's Place and old Ely, plus a hand-drawn floor plan of the whole row dating back to 1500 that made Ewan mutter imprecations and devout thanks. 'I need to go and photocopy this. Do you want a copy, Clare?'

'Yes, please,' I said. Then I let out a satisfied sigh of my own. I had found a survey plan of Almoner's Close and the High Street, with notes in all the margins and all the buildings marked with names.

'So much space,' mused Ewan, his finger tracing the lines of the streets outside. He glanced out of the back window. 'All the land has been filled in now. I wonder what it looked like before.'

I could have told him. The map pretty well matched the sixteenth-century vision I'd had. On balance, however, I thought he'd probably had enough weird stuff from me today. 'Look, it lists the residences.' I peered at the cramped writing and located No. 4. 'Thomas Woodman, master carpenter.' As I said it, I felt a sharp jab in my chest, as if it was a name I should know.

Ewan bent over it. 'That's your house, Clare, not this one. There was a Master William Hewitt, stonemason, next door at No. 3. It doesn't surprise me. Cathedrals take a deal of stone, and they were building this one for three hundred years or so. There would have been a lot of work for your carpenter too. The canons didn't stint themselves when it came to furnishings.'

'Canons?' I said, but I wasn't really listening. My heart was thumping wildly as I correlated *master carpenter* with the sawing and hammering sounds I'd heard during that brief flashback. And there had also been the image of the boy whittling in the window seat of my living room the other day. Thomas the singing boy had described himself as the son of the house. Maybe that had been him, named for his father.

'When Henry the Eighth dissolved the monastery, they kept the cathedral, but the principal buildings were turned into houses for the canons of the cathedral,' explained Ewan, bringing me back to the present.

I remembered the books about Ely. 'Oh yes, I read about that. The whole town really did exist for the cathedral, didn't it? Oh, I could study these for hours.'

'Me too,' said Ewan. 'Sadly, I've got a meeting with the surveyor that I need to prepare data for.'

'I should be getting back to work too.'

Ewan left and I put the plans away with regret. I had the feeling Leonard wouldn't have minded me happily poring over them all day, but I mustn't give way to temptation. I'd found out part of what I wanted to know, at any rate. I knew what my house had been and who had lived and worked there back in the mid-1500s.

But I still didn't know why I was mixed up with it all.

★   ★   ★

'We've got in. Want to see? It must be the most unique priest hole ever.'

I looked up from the computer, registering from the mellow rays slanting through the window that it must be close to five o'clock. Ewan was standing in the doorway, hazel eyes bright, his T-shirt and jeans covered in brick dust and flecks of white paint.

Leonard was on the phone in the far room and wouldn't want to be disturbed. I followed Ewan downstairs into the old kitchen.

'See? The back wall of the cupboard looks like brick, feels like brick, *is* brick, but it's only a thin layer attached to a wooden panel, which then swings out. There are concealed catches at the top and bottom. It's a beautiful piece of work. I'm betting there was collusion with next door — the stonemason and the carpenter, remember? Do you want to go in?'

'Not especially,' I said, shuddering as I looked at the gap behind the false back of the cupboard and the real end wall of the house. Such a narrow space in which to live a life.

'I'd love to date it,' murmured Ewan. 'Priest holes were used for Protestants during Mary's time and Catholics before and after. I wonder which this was.'

I turned away abruptly, remembering that paralysing fear at the entrance. If it was like that there, it must be worse actually inside. I really didn't want to experience that in depth. 'What are you going to use this room for?' I said, changing the subject.

There was a tiny moment of surprise, then, 'It was pencilled in for storage, but after listening to you and Leonard on the subject of researchers, I'm thinking of designating it a common room instead, as it's so handy for the new reading room. It was already a kitchen, so the plumbing is there, though it may need updating. We can easily put in a fridge and kettle and microwave. Then it can be used for the eating of sandwiches and drinking of tea by readers, safely away from your precious books.'

My mood lifted instantly. 'That's a fabulous idea!'

He grinned at me, pleased. 'Glad you approve.'

'Oh, I do.' He reddened slightly. 'Clare, I've been meaning to ask — are you busy this evening? It's quiz night at the Minster Tavern. The guys here make up a team. You'd be very welcome to join in with us. The pub does excellent fish and chips.'

Real life. That was one of the things I'd moved away from London to find. I needed to interact with other people, to rebuild my confidence. I needed to concentrate on me again. My mood lifted even further. 'Thank you, I'd like that. What time? If it's straight from work, I'll need fifteen minutes to change.'

'That's not a problem. Some of the lads nip home first and then come back with wives or girlfriends. I go from here. I'm happy to wait for you.'

There was the tiniest pause. Was I supposed to ask? I did anyway. 'Is your wife or girlfriend not interested in pub quiz evenings, then?'

'I'm divorced. She . . . she didn't like the long separations when I was on a job.'

'I'm sorry.'

'These things happen.' Ewan shrugged, but his smile had slipped and I could sense the hurt ran deep.

* * *

I'd been ready several minutes when Ewan knocked on the front door. 'Sorry, Clare — I've mislaid my mobile, and I'm away for the weekend, so I need it. I'll be with you soon.'

'Well, I'm all ready to go, so if you'd

like another pair of eyes to help look, I could come with you.'

'The more the merrier, if you don't mind. Thanks. Goodness only knows what I've done with it.'

'Come in while I get my jacket on.' I turned to lift it down from the row of hooks.

'Nice flowers. Were they the ones that were delivered the other day?' asked Ewan, nodding towards the bouquet.

I glanced across. 'Yes, but they weren't from my mother at all. The place where I used to work sent them as a settling-in present. I did think it was rather odd, Mum paying out perfectly good money for flowers when she could just dig me up a clump from the garden and put them in a pot. She's dreadful like that. Every time we moved, she'd bring half the previous rectory garden with her. The one she and Dad are in at the moment, she can walk the full circuit of the lawn and tell you where in the country each plant originally came from.'

Ewan grinned. 'Your father's a vicar?'

'He's a career vicar. He's worked himself up to rural dean now. He was ecstatic when I got the job here. I give it another month at the most before they pay me a visit. Then Mum will fill my larder with cake and pies and wheels of cheese, and Dad will wander over to the cathedral and accidentally make friends with everyone in a clerical collar who misguidedly comes into view.'

I locked up and we returned next door. I followed Ewan into his office, where he gazed around with that irritation we all feel when we've done something dumb. 'I suppose you've tried ringing yourself, have you?' I asked.

'Yes, but the phone was on silent because I was in that meeting with the surveyor.'

There wasn't much room in his office with all the furniture he'd crammed in. I leaned against the wall out of the way, shutting my eyes and thinking myself into his shoes. I knew how he worked by now. He was tidy in the face of all the confusion in the house. He did things at once; didn't let them slide. I could almost see him shaking hands with the surveyor, seeing him out, then coming straight back in here to type his meeting notes into the computer while they were fresh in his mind.

'What did you do after you'd finished with the surveyor?' I asked. 'Put papers away? Write down bullet-point reminders?'

His shout startled my eyes open. 'That's it! Clare, you're a genius. I needed something out of the filing cabinet, and put the phone down . . . ' He broke off, stretched up, and felt around on top of the pile of reports balanced on the filing cabinet. He looked at me sheepishly, the mobile now in his hand. 'Thanks.'

I grinned as I pushed myself away from the wall. 'You're welcome. I always find it helps to retrace my steps if I mislay anything.'

Out of nowhere, I felt a strong waft

of approval. Bright eyes and a brisk nod. I blinked.

'Ready for the pub, then?' said Ewan.

'Yes,' I said, blinking again. Now. The sooner the better.

6

We talked about Leonard's library as we walked to the pub. Ewan already knew the collection was valuable in monetary terms. I tried to explain how important it also was in the world of early music research.

'Broadly speaking, the field of early music comprises the Medieval period between 500 and 1400 A.D., the Renaissance period from 1400 to 1600, and Leonard also includes the Baroque, which is 1600 to 1760.'

He nodded. 'Got you.'

'A lot of the material can be found elsewhere,' I said, 'but here in Almoner's Place it's all together, a huge concentration of work on the subject as well as many actual manuscripts themselves. We don't have any ancient instruments, just the printed matter. Leonard is more about theory and development, and besides, instruments need space. There are several working early music museums around if people want to hear what the music sounded like in its original form.'

'I'd guess the limitations of the instruments had a knock-on effect on the compositions,' he said. 'Have you visited any of the museums?'

'Oh yes, and played some of the instruments, but I'm not a musician. I like singing and I like the music, that's all. The point is, Leonard is one of the leading experts in the field. Researchers are going to be in heaven once they get access. One of the tasks I have to do, as well as cataloguing everything, is to put a retrieval system in place so when people request an item, I go to the right shelf or cabinet or occasional table to get it for them. Everything will be computerised, of course, but I'll also put an old-fashioned holding ticket in the item's space until I return it when the reader has finished. That's mostly as a visual check, though it'll also be handy if there's a power cut, and so Leonard doesn't panic when he sees something missing. The procedures will need to be approved, but Newrigg are leaving the system design to me. No point employing a dog and barking yourself.'

Ewan listened thoughtfully. The evening was warm and people around us were Friday-relaxed. 'You'll do the retrieving yourself?' he queried.

'Certainly to begin with.' I grinned at him. 'I'm in heaven, too. This is my dream job. Also, I think Leonard needs someone he can trust during the early stages. He's not going to find it easy, sharing his library.'

When we reached the Minster Tavern, it was dense with leaded windows and crowded with hanging baskets. I wrinkled my nose. It seemed too nice an evening to be inside.

Ewan laughed at my expression. 'Do you want a bit more of a wander first? There's plenty of time.'

I was tempted. Then I looked down

the road and saw the narrow triangle of grass where I'd felt so dreadfully cold the first day I arrived. 'Maybe not,' I said.

He looked at me with understanding.

'This is ridiculous,' I said with a groan. 'I'm perfectly normal. I'm really ordinary. And yet . . . ' I glanced down the road again.

'And yet something on Palace Green freaked you out the other day and you don't know if it's going to do it again.'

His matter-of-fact words fell in front of me like black typewritten letters clattering onto an empty page. 'Yes.'

He looked reflectively at the green. 'Can't ignore it forever.'

I thought of all my mistakes with Jonathan. 'You'd be surprised,' I muttered.

'You said I helped you through your initial shock at the priest hole. I'm willing to haul you out again. At least you'll know one way or the other if there's something there.'

So we continued walking. I told him

how my parents had planned to visit Ely when I was small. 'But when we got here I suddenly started screaming — within sight of the cathedral — and I wouldn't stop until we'd left the town completely. I'm trying not to let that influence me.'

Ewan laughed. 'Dead right. My cousin's little boy sobs dementedly, purely because he can. I swear he gets a kick out of seeing us all rush around trying to work out what's wrong.'

He guided me over to look at the cannon. The plaque said it was captured from the Russians in Sebastopol and given to the people of Ely by Queen Victoria in 1860 after the Crimean War.

'That was nice of her,' I commented. 'I wonder what she thought the people of Ely would do with it?'

Ewan was looking at me oddly. 'What is it?' I asked.

'Nothing. I thought you might put your hand on the cannon, that's all.'

'Why would I do that?' I asked, bewildered.

'You did with the cupboard wall when you wanted to find out about it.'

I stared, thinking back. 'I suppose I did. But it wouldn't work with this.'

'How do you know?'

'I just do.' I rested my hand on the cannon. Even given the lingering warmth of the day, the metal was dull and cold. 'Nothing,' I said. 'Objects are different from buildings.'

'Probably just as well, or you'd be really freaked out with everything you touched wanting to tell you its story.'

I shuddered involuntarily. 'Don't. That would be like Italy all over again.'

'What do you mean?'

'It was awful. I went over to Europe on a travelling scholarship after I got my doctorate. All sorts of places: Paris, Lyons, Rome, Venice, Florence ... I was terrifically excited by the trip and probably not eating and drinking very sensibly. Basically I got so dizzy and saturated with the history all around me that I couldn't even concentrate, let alone do any work. I think I actually was ill, but I was trying not to give into it because I didn't want to waste the opportunities I'd been offered.'

Ewan looked sympathetic. 'You ended up making yourself worse?'

'You got it. I kept on trying, because I wasn't so bad first thing in the mornings. But one time in Florence I felt so dreadful, I just stopped right there in the Piazza della Signoria. Looking back, I suppose it was a panic attack. Whatever it was, it terrified me. I just couldn't think what to do next. I couldn't walk. I could barely talk. I remember wondering if my lungs could really manage to breathe by themselves.'

'Practically always,' said Ewan. 'What did you do?'

'This is going to sound really wimpish. I rang Mum.'

The whirling kaleidoscope of images came to mind again. I remembered doubling up in a corner, leaning against the wall of the Palazzo Vecchio gasping for breath and fumbling my phone out of my bag. It had been a warm day, and the stones of the wall had pressed into the bare skin of my shoulders. But it hadn't cooled me down; it had made me worse.

'Sweetheart,' Mum had said, 'for goodness sake, just stop for half an hour and buy yourself an ice-cream. You know that works when you get in a tizzy.' Her familiar common sense had spurred me into leaving the safety of the wall and finding a gelateria.

'Oh!' I said now. I stopped dead, enlightened. *Leaving the wall*. I *did* do the hand thing with buildings. I did it a lot. I'd done it here at the cathedral. I'd done it at No. 4. And I had presumably done it when I was travelling in Europe. If I was sensitive to a building's atmosphere, no wonder I had got overloaded. I had probably been touching every wall I went past.

'You rang your mother from Italy? What did she say?'

'She told me to have an ice-cream.'

'Splendid idea,' said Ewan, looking around.

'Yes, but listen. I was touching the walls there. I've only just realised how much I do it. When I arrived in Ely, for example, the first thing I did was to put my hand against No. 4 before I went inside. I wonder if that's how I knew where everything was.'

'It's not the daftest thing I've ever heard. Has that happened anywhere else? The *déjà vu* feeling, I mean.'

'No, mostly I just get feelings. I'd never worked it out that analytically before. It could explain what happened in Italy. There's a lot of atmosphere there. Do you know, that makes me feel much better about myself.' If it was true, it meant I wasn't a failure in the real world after all. I could have coped with life even before Jon came along to blind me with love and sweep me up in his train — I'd simply been unwise about not filtering out the emotional hit. That was why my travelling scholarship had started to go wrong; I hadn't known enough about myself. I felt ten times lighter, as if an invisible pressure had been lifted off my shoulders. 'Thank you,' I said.

Ewan gave me a grin. 'I have no idea what you're talking about, but you're very welcome.'

We strolled on. I'd forgotten about searching for the cold spot. I stooped to read a tiny oval plaque on a wall, low down at pavement level:

'Near this place on 16th October 1555, William Wolsey, Constable of Wellney, Upwell, Outwell and Robert Pygot, painter from Wisbech, were burnt at the stake for their Christian Faith.'

'How horrible,' I said.

Ewan looked at it sombrely. '1555? Queen Mary, right? Wanted everyone to be Catholic. It could be why our priest hole was constructed. They were pretty dark days.' He gave a reflective sigh. 'Ready for a beer yet?'

I nodded. 'Yes.'

And then I found the cold place, the place of dread. I instinctively gripped Ewan's arm as my stomach swooped with terror.

'I'm here.' His hand covered mine, warm and encouraging.

This time I battled the soul-cold fear and caught unvoiced words behind it. A woman's voice. A nearly familiar presence. A driving sense of urgency.

No. No, no, no. They're coming for me. But I'm not one. It's just a different way of looking. I would never harm. My neighbours know that.

And then, much stronger: *I must protect the girl.*

'Can I help at all?' That was Ewan again.

I broke free, stumbling forward. 'I'm okay,' I said.

'You don't look it.'

I met his eyes. 'I'm nearly okay. There was something there — something that happened once, something bad. But I need to . . . to process it. I need to think about it somewhere quiet.' I gave a shiver. 'Not yet, though. For now I'd like that beer.'

The pub was blissfully normal, boisterously noisy, decorated with old prints and framed newspaper cuttings, and smelling most wonderfully of fish and chips. By the time I had eaten an enormous plateful, I felt in tune with the world again and able to contribute to the quiz.

I answered a literary question and a music question, and translated a Latin motto, enabling the rest of the team to answer an armed forces question. Honour satisfied, I thought. Between rounds, I examined the cuttings on the walls. The one immediately behind me was about a spooky sighting in the Minster Tavern itself.

'You didn't tell me there was a resident ghost here,' I said.

Ewan laughed. 'If you believe the tourist board, Ely has a ghost in every pub. In this case, though, the woman behind the bar swears she sometimes sees a man sitting in one of the chairs when she comes in to clean in the morning. When she looks again, he's disappeared.'

I nodded. 'That's certainly my experience with men and cleaning.'

The team chuckled and ordered another round.

I carried on reading. The cuttings were all of a piece, about unexplained happenings and murders and disappearances and charlatans being exposed. And then I froze. Another newspaper facsimile, this time a penny dreadful list of local witches over the centuries; and there at the bottom a last throwaway line, torn unevenly so I couldn't read the end: *In 1570 a charge of witchcraft was also made against Johanna Woodman b —*

Johanna Woodman? The name leapt out at me. Could she have been a relative of Thomas Woodman, who had lived and worked in my house in the sixteenth century? The date was right. I remembered the old woman I'd seen carding wool in the Almoner's Place garden, the one with the piercing blue eyes. Had that been Johanna Woodman? I was filled again with the dread urgency I'd felt on Palace Green. Had that been her voice? Had she seen people coming for her? Was that why she'd been rooted to the spot, whispering *no, no, no* in disbelief? The same fear took hold of me. I couldn't let it rest now. What had happened to her? I needed to find out more, and quickly. I surreptitiously slid my phone out of my bag and brought up Google.

★   ★   ★

Ewan walked back with me after the quiz. 'Just to see you home while you're still new to the area,' he said.

'That's kind, but I can hardly miss with the cathedral there. It's not even properly dark yet. You said you were going away for the weekend. I don't want to make you late.'

'I wouldn't be going this time of night, would I? Besides, I'm over the limit for driving. I'll leave first thing tomorrow. It's not urgent; I'm only going home. I need to check on my house, and there are . . . there are one or two other bits of business I need to see to.'

'Oh, right. Where do you live?'

'My house is in Edgware near my parents. I'm renting it out, and the tenant says one of the doors is sticking, which is why I need to visit. For the duration of this contract I've got a place on Fore Hill.'

'That all sounds quite complicated.'

'It's the nature of the job,' Ewan said matter-of-factly. 'When I'm away for long periods, I'd rather a tenant covered my mortgage repayments than have them come out of my wages. Here's Almoner's Close. I'll see you on Monday. Have a good weekend.'

I smiled. 'Thank you. Have a good weekend yourself.'

As he walked away, I thought I heard him murmur, 'Chance would be a fine thing.'

★   ★   ★

I'd googled 'Johanna Woodman' while I was in the pub and got thousands of Woodman references. I now googled

'Johanna Woodman witch trial' and got rather less, but still far too many to check out.

The obvious thing to do, unconventional as it might seem, was to ask the singing boys about Johanna Woodman. It wasn't a line of research that would stand up in an academic paper, but if I accepted I wasn't going mad and that I did have some sort of empathy with people who had lived in my house centuries before, it would be a useful shortcut. After the shock of finding that torn witch-trial cutting in the pub, I needed to ask now, before I went to bed. I needed to know.

I started at the top of the house. 'Who was Johanna?' I asked in the bedroom. There was no reply. Thomas and Robert were evidently off about their business. I repeated the question in the living room. Still nothing.

Ha, that would serve me right for thinking it would be easy. Perhaps the boys would be back tomorrow. I went down to the kitchen to make a last mug of tea, needing to settle myself. My eyes were drawn to the nail where I'd automatically hung the ring of keys that first day. I put my hand up to it, touching the iron of the nail and the blackened oak of the beam. My fingertips met the tiny ridges running all along the grain of the wood. Assurance rolled through me. This was *right*. I felt as liquid as water and as solid as flint. It was the weirdest sensation, but I really *was* connected to the house.

'Who was Johanna Woodman?' I said aloud.

There was a pause, then a gathering of information stretching down the years and rolling back again to me, coming not as words but as knowledge, arriving in my head all of a piece. Johanna Woodman, the house told me, was the master carpenter's mother, the singing boy Thomas's grandmother. She had come to the house as a bride, then made the running of it over to her daughter-in-law on her son's marriage.

As was the custom, she had contin.
to live with the household. She was 'the
woman who knew'.

I stumbled on that. *The woman who
knew?* What did that mean? The
woman who knew what? But it was all I
was getting. The house didn't seem able
to help further. I was left with a
succession of images: shrewd blue eyes
and a white coif; people knocking at the
door and her wrapping a shawl around
practical, capable shoulders and following them; pots of honey or a rabbit or
maybe even a loaf of bread left on the
doorstep by way of a thank-you.

I took my hand down from the beam,
disoriented and with a strange fizzing in
my veins. Had I really just communed
with the house? I must have done. I
couldn't have imagined the whole thing
out of nowhere. So where had it got
me?

It had got me to Johanna Woodman,
a real person living centuries ago in my
house. A woman who 'knew'. But what
had happened to her?

7

I woke to metallic clattering and cheerful shouts. Traders were setting up the Saturday market over in the High Street. I stretched luxuriously, feeling the cotton sheets smooth against my legs, enjoying the way the early morning light played across the low ceiling, very happy to be in bed at the top of this old house revelling in the thought of two days with no one to consider except myself.

I chuckled. Next door, Leonard was probably equally thankful for the very same thing, but whereas he would blissfully potter around his empty library for the whole weekend, I had more ambitious plans. No more hanging around waiting for the phone to ring. Not ever again. I was going to visit the cathedral properly, and the market, and the museum.

I would have adored a lovely long study of Leonard's old maps of Ely too, but I wasn't going to disturb his peace; and in any case, he had lost the key to the chest. I had replaced the maps inside after I'd looked at them before, realising too late that the 'snick' I heard as the lid closed meant that the mechanism had re-locked. The thought of causing more damage by opening it with the pliers again made my stomach turn.

Find the key, said a cheeky voice in my head. *You've got Mistress Johanna's gift. Use it.*

About to throw off the sheet and leap out of bed, I froze at the intrusion. 'Out of my bedroom!' I said. 'Now!'

Laughter rang in my mind, fading as the ghost-boys left.

I lay still while my heart rate subsided to normal. I was going to have to get used to this. I didn't think the boys meant any harm — certainly not voyeurism; they were just here. Or not here, as the case might be. Would I get to know other past inhabitants of the house if I stayed in Almoner's Place long enough? Or was it simply that these lads were stronger because they were so full of life, so joyous and mischievous?

I flicked through memories of other old houses we'd lived in. There had been a lot. Thinking about them, I suppose I'd always been aware of their different atmospheres, but apart from that one time in Yorkshire with the ghost-children, I'd never felt people before. Neither had I seen visions or ghosts in any of the ecclesiastical or college libraries I'd worked in, and they were surely old enough to have any number of memorable characters.

So it had to be the past inhabitants themselves who were the guiding factor in whether I could interact with them. Maybe they had to want me to. I couldn't work out whether this was comforting or not. I didn't like the idea of not being in control of the situation. I was only just taking my life back, building it around *me* rather than around occasional moments with Jonathan. I wanted to stay in charge, thank you.

I stretched again. Time to get up and start the weekend rolling. A quick shower first, then I'd see if any of the market stalls were doing breakfast. Treat myself.

At the back of my mind, though, the issue the boys' words had raised bided its time, refusing to go away.

You've got Mistress Johanna's gift. Use it.

What did they mean?

*   *   *

The street market was raucous, bustling and cheerful. I sauntered along the lines of stalls, buying a scrap of cheese here, tasting a cube of bread there, inhaling a bursting aroma of summer flowers on the corner. I was debating with myself the necessity of buying both olive bread and tomato-and-herb bread when my mobile rang.

'Instruments of the devil,' remarked

the stallholder philosophically. 'Aren't you going to answer it?'

I looked at the display. It was Jonathan. No doubt he was snatching a few minutes while he dropped his daughter at her ballet lesson. I used to be grateful for these crumbs of time. Now I was unsettled that he was still trying to make contact, even though I'd moved away. 'No,' I said, thumbing the answerphone button. 'People should know it's dangerous to interrupt a woman when she's shopping. I'll have both loaves, please.'

I tore an end off the olive bread and sent a photo of myself eating it to Mum. *See? I'm eating. Happy?*

She emailed back, telling me to buy cheese to go with it. Or better still, a bacon roll. *Top idea, Mum.* I found one at a stall and devoured it with relish, though it had made my fingers so very greasy that I needed to wash them before I continued with the Great Weekend Plan. It was easiest to do this at home, so I went back and put away my shopping at the same time. Out of habit, I switched on my laptop to check my emails.

There was one from Jonathan saying sorry he'd missed me on the phone and it was just to ask a business question, really. Did Leonard still have that ornamented setting of the *Kyrie Eleison* they'd both bid on last year? Had he finished with it? Jonathan had a client who wanted to buy it.

'I don't know,' I typed back curtly, 'and it would be inappropriate for me to raise the question. Please don't ask me anything like this again. I work for Leonard now, not for you.'

I sent the reply unsigned, cross with him for disturbing my weekend, and *very* cross with him for assuming I was still enough of his creature to intercede for him. I shut the computer down again and went back outside.

Ely was a very pretty city. I'd not lived here a week yet, and I was already feeling proprietary about the mix of buildings and the sense of permanence.

At the museum I read the information boards, paid the entry charge and went in — and only just stopped myself in time from laying my hand against the wall. I really *did* do that automatically. Today I wouldn't. The main part of the museum, the board had said, was housed inside the thirteenth-century gaol. I could do without several hundred years of misery flooding me on a lovely sunny Saturday!

It was a standard town museum, the displays designed for entertainment as much as for education. Nothing for the serious scholar, but as a run-through of Ely's history it served its purpose. There were diagrams of the encircling marshy fens, not drained until after Cromwell's ascendance. There were drawings of the original monastery in wood, rebuilt in soaring stone by the Normans for the greater glory of God. It looked as if neither time nor money had ever been an object where the cathedral was concerned. The world-famous Octagon, for example, had taken eighteen years to construct.

Then there was information on the dissolution under Henry VIII and an explanation of how the monastery was re-founded as a cathedral church, with the King's School incorporated into the rest. It was all very much as I'd expected.

In which complacent frame of mind, I rounded a corner — and stopped with an enormous thump of my heart as the headline 'WITCHES' blazed out at me in shrieking black capitals from an ochre display board. 'Idiot,' I scolded myself in a mutter. 'It's only a display.' Even so, I took several very deep breaths before looking more closely at the board.

Witchcraft in Tudor times, it appeared, was a blanket term used for anything people of an inflexible disposition didn't understand. In 1542, the first ever Witchcraft Act had made it a crime punishable by death to use supernatural powers to find money or treasure, or to kill, or to make people fall in love with you. If you were found guilty, in addition to executing you, your goods and chattel were forfeited.

The possibility of being hung *and* dispossessed was a pretty good reason to keep quiet, in my view. The act was repealed five years later, but another one was passed under Elizabeth I in 1563. Now the death sentence only applied if actual harm was caused. Lesser crimes were punished by a year of imprisonment, presumably in this very gaol, if the witchfinders had been active in Ely. It came to me in a nauseous rush that I'd been right: this *was* what the hurrying words I'd heard on Palace Green had meant.

I'm not one. It's just a different way of looking. I would never harm. My neighbours know that.

The speaker had been accused of being a witch. That had to be it. Had she been warned by a neighbour while she was out, perhaps? Was that why she'd stood long enough in that place for her fear to stick to the air? Or was it because she'd seen soldiers, or whatever the equivalent of the constabulary was in those days, looking for her?

I walked another few steps to the next display board, only subliminally registering the change in the light levels, the alteration in the stonework. And now, here in the old gaol, there was suddenly more. The woman's voice was back. Stronger. Ringing in my ears.

I must stay safe. Dear my Lord, I must stay safe. I must teach the child to protect herself so none suspect. My line. My duty. I must be strong for her.

The words lodged in my chest along with the fear. They crowded my head, more urgent than ever. I looked around wildly. Why was I hearing them? I wasn't touching the walls, yet it was as if she was right here beside me. Johanna. I knew it was Johanna. The aura that I'd picked up from communing with the house last night infused her words and melded with my bones. I would know her anywhere now.

A family group pushed past me, the

children eager to read about witches and trials. They pointed with glee to a picture. I spun away from it, the crude woodcut of three women hanging from a gibbet sickening me. I was shaken and disoriented, the food I'd eaten turning rancid in my stomach.

Johanna! What was she doing here in the gaol? What had happened to her? I hurtled home, barely making it without retching, hearing the echoes of other racing footsteps, years gone by, keeping pace with mine.

I'd just reached the safety of Almoner's Place and unlocked my door when my phone rang again. I got it out of my bag with shaking hands, answering at the same time as seeing it was Jonathan. *Again.*

'Go away,' I screamed, not giving him time to say anything. 'Just leave me alone!' I left the phone on the table and huddled into a ball in my kitchen with my eyes screwed shut and my hands tight over my ears.

After a minute, or five, or ten, I

became aware of Gregorian plainsong, a faint high thread of sound, pure and peaceful. I let myself uncurl, opened my eyes, and focused on my sane normal world in sane normal time. I shakily brewed tea, hot and strong, and took it up to my living room. Earlier this week I had seen a vision of this room as it had been in the late sixteenth century. I wanted to see it again. I needed to look at the people properly.

I sat down, wrapped my hands around the mug, and summoned my resolution. 'May I see the room again, please?' I asked.

And just like that — there it was. After the agitation of the gaol and the terror of my instinctive hurtle back here, the calm of this scene was both reassuring and bewildering. Was this before the words had been spoken that I'd heard in the gaol or after? I had no idea. I sipped my tea and committed the scene to memory.

An older woman and a middle-aged one were sewing comfortably on the cushioned bench, talking, though I couldn't hear what was being said. The boy Thomas, cheeky and fair-haired, was whittling on the window seat, and a child was playing on the floor with her doll. I drew in my breath sharply. Both women's heads were covered, but the child had pale blonde hair in a shade I knew rather well, and blue eyes identical to those of her grandmother. The older woman was Johanna Woodman. She was the woman in the yard, the fear on the green, the voice in the gaol.

'I don't understand,' I said as the picture faded, but I was fooling myself. I was beginning to think I understood only too well. In my thirty years on this earth, I had met very few people with hair of the same unusual colour as my own. All of them had been related to me.

Johanna, Thomas, the girl playing with her doll on the floor . . . These people were my ancestors.

* * *

I spent the rest of the day reading everything I could find about Elizabethan Ely. I devoured the guide books I'd bought at the cathedral. I rushed out to the library to hurriedly borrow local history books. I browsed pages and pages on the internet. I saturated myself with this one slice of the past. Maybe that was why my dream that night was so vivid.

I dreamt I was the child, Alys, accompanying her grandmother on an errand. The details in the dream were so accurate that I felt the weight of the basket Alys was carrying, I smelled the ox dung on the air, and my pattens slipped with hers on the straw laid over the greasy cobbles. Johanna talked to Alys as we went. I couldn't hear the words; I could only sense Alys's reaction. When we reached our destination, I was bidden to be quiet and watch as Johanna Woodman, neat in her shawl and snowy coif, knocked on the low wooden door of a cottage. As Alys, I obediently stood out of the way once we were inside the simple dwelling; but the part of me that was aware I was dreaming gasped out loud as I saw Johanna rest her hand on the wall as she listened to her neighbour's story.

I couldn't take my eyes off that hand. Joanna asked questions of the neighbour, who fidgeted continuously, darting to a drawer, a closet, and then finally to a low cupboard where he triumphantly unearthed a small pouch. This was evidently what he had been looking for. It was also, Alys's satisfaction told me, why her grandmother had been summoned. She was the woman who knew. Grateful tears started in the man's eyes. Johanna refused payment with a slight movement of her hand and a smile, and we left the cottage to return home. Upon which I woke, sweat-soaked and trembling, trying to make sense of what I'd experienced.

Johanna and I were both able to connect with houses — was that the gift? But I didn't see what she'd done to locate the man's pouch. And I was no nearer finding out what had happened to her in the gaol. *Please don't tell me she was executed. Not now I know her. Please.* I couldn't bear it.

8

Sunday bells dancing on the town air woke me. In contrast to yesterday's cheerful bustle, today all was calm when I opened my window. There was an email on my laptop from Mel, the contact for the local choir, saying she was going to be at the service in the cathedral this morning, and would I like to meet her for coffee in the refectory café afterwards, perhaps? She added that the café did a rather fine latte and an excellent ginger cake.

'Sold,' I emailed back. 'An offer I can't refuse.' Real life. I loved it.

Cathedral services always pull out all the stops. This one had rolling phrases and soaring music and was beautiful, soothing and uplifting all at once. It also had a distinctly sixteenth-century harmony in the upper register that I thought I might be the only person to hear.

It may sound trite, but I was suddenly filled with hope. I could do this. I could make a new life here in Ely. I could put Jon behind me and consign those memories to lessons learned. I could find out about my ancestors. I could even survive the inevitable visit from Mum and Dad. I sang along with my ghost-choristers and felt my cares drop away and a new sense of purpose settle into their place.

Mel, the administrator for the local choir, was a joy. She was a little older than me, lively and enthusiastic, with a wicked sense of humour. She signed me up, invited me to dinner on Tuesday, and gave me a piece to learn for Wednesday evening's practice that fortunately I was already familiar with. Real life *was* wonderful. This was what I would be concentrating on from now on.

Strolling back home through the sunshine, saturated with gingerbread and good feeling, I caught sight of Ewan Matlock on the other side of the street. 'Hi,' I said, crossing the road. 'I thought you were going to be away for the weekend.'

'Hi, Clare. I was. I came back early.'

I studied his face. 'You don't have to tell me about it if you don't want to.'

He gave me a strained smile. 'What are you doing for lunch?'

★ ★ ★

We went down to the river. I had mentioned I had two different sorts of bread and the makings of a substantial salad at home, but he said there are some stories that require a beer in the telling. Also roast chicken.

The pub, when we got there, didn't have a table free for half an hour, so we walked along by the water's edge, watching the ducks and swans and eating ice-creams. I think Ewan just needed something to do with his hands.

'My dad's a GP,' he began. 'My

mum's a teacher. It makes for a very moral household.'

'You should try being brought up by a vicar,' I said, laughing.

'I think that's why I'm telling you this. I don't usually.'

I chased a long drip of salted caramel with my tongue. 'Go on, then. I promise not to pass judgement.'

'I have two younger brothers. I also have a younger sister.'

'You're very lucky. I wish I did.' I wondered suddenly if that was why I'd connected with the ghost children up in Yorkshire — because I was lonely. *Stop it, Clare. Don't get distracted. Listen to Ewan.*

'Anyway, there's only a year between me and Anthony. Chris and Jenny are younger. I'm very fond of them, but they don't come into this.' He finished his ice-cream with a crunch, wiped his fingers, and looked for somewhere to throw away the serviette. I took it from him and dropped it into my bag along with mine.

'Anthony and I used to do everything together,' he said. He stopped and gazed over the water, hurt twisting his face.

'Is he a civil engineer too?' I asked.

Ewan gave a short laugh. 'Anthony is a lawyer, a successful one. That's part of the problem.'

'Having a successful lawyer in the family doesn't *sound* like a problem,' I said with some caution.

'A successful lawyer,' he said, addressing the swans that were swimming down to investigate us, 'is a far better catch as far as marriage is concerned than a hands-on civil engineer.'

I winced. 'Your brother poached your girlfriend?'

He made an uncoordinated movement. 'No, he poached my wife.'

'Oh, Ewan.' I impulsively put my hand on his arm.

The swans gave up on us. Ewan watched them glide towards another couple, strolling along. 'What made it worse was that Gina was originally

142

going out with him before she married me.'

'Oh, Ewan!'

He tucked my hand into his arm. I'm not totally sure he knew what he was doing, but he evidently needed the reassurance of friendly human contact. I didn't mind. I needed friendly human contact too.

He glanced at his watch. 'We should be going back if we want that table.'

We turned and he started again. 'I was doing my degree at Imperial College. Anthony was at Westminster Law School. We'd meet up fairly frequently, often with girlfriends in tow. Sometimes the ladies got on, sometimes they didn't. You know the sort of thing.'

'I do indeed.'

Ewan sighed. 'And then there was Gina. Gina was beautiful, reading Art History, and very fond of Anthony.'

'With you so far,' I said.

'She spent Christmas with us, took umbrage at Anthony going off to play in a squash tournament with Chris, got hammered on the sherry she was supposed to be drip-feeding into the trifle, and ambushed me under the mistletoe on the back porch when no one was looking.'

'Ooops.'

He slanted a look down at me. 'I, incidentally, had just been dumped, so wasn't objecting to having my *amour propre* restored.'

'What happened?'

'Nothing that time, apart from a rather steamy kiss. But she also stayed with us over the long summer holidays. I was on an engineering placement for most of it. My coming home coincided with Anthony doing work experience with a solicitor pal of Dad's.'

'Double ooops.'

'Correct. Let's just say that for several years, relations between Anthony and me have not been what you might call cordial.'

I narrowed my eyes. This Gina sounded like a spoilt little witch. 'Did the circumstance of a civil engineer graduating well ahead of a law student come into it at all?' I asked.

'Clever, aren't you? That never entered my head at the time. I just thought what a smart bloke I was to have a stunner like Gina preferring me over Anthony.'

We reached the pub and were shown to a bijou table for two overlooking the river. It was a nice view, but wasted on Ewan. He was so far in the past, they could have put us indoors next to the coats and he wouldn't have noticed.

He studied the menu now in a way that I suspected meant he wasn't really seeing it. 'You know the worst thing?' he asked.

'Nope. Tell me.'

'I still have no idea, for all that time we were together, whether there was ever anything there for her, or whether she was just marking off the days until Anthony was qualified and earning enough to support her.' He said it casually, but beneath the words were enough complexes to keep Freud in business for six months.

I rubbed my nose, trying to think of the right thing to say. 'It sounds to me as if you've both been had, but you escaped.'

He sighed. 'Maybe.'

I tried again. 'I'm assuming there were no children?'

'No. I'd have liked a family, but she wasn't keen. She manages an art gallery and loves it. Pregnancy would cramp her style.'

'Did she make you happy when you were together?'

'Yes. I thought she felt the same.'

'She probably did. Right up until you started leaving her alone for long periods on bigger projects. That was what you said the other day, wasn't it?'

He gazed at the menu again, creasing the corner, folding it into narrow pleats. I reached across and stilled his hand. 'Do you want Gina back?' I asked.

'God, no,' he said, looking at me with a horrified face. 'But I'd quite like to stop feeling so angry and used. Plus, whenever I go back to Mum and Dad's and they're there too . . . '

I could guess. Gina would be all cat and cream and elegant clothes and little sly glances out of the corner of her eye to see if Ewan was madly jealous. Anthony would be slightly embarrassed, defensively pleased with himself, harbouring just a lingering insecurity in case there was still a spark between Gina and Ewan. After all, Gina had left him once for his brother. Gina, of course, would lap that up too.

'Oh!' I said, suddenly getting it. 'Oh, yes, I understand now. What you need to do is make friends with your brother again. Proper friends, like you used to be. You'll both feel masses better, and Gina will be furious.' I looked at him. 'I think you'll be happier too, won't you? You said you were very close when you were growing up. You must have missed him.'

Ewan stared at me for so long that I had plenty of time to enumerate to myself all the occasions before now on which my mouth had outstripped my brain. 'Um, sorry,' I mumbled. 'None of my business. Ignore me.'

'But you're right,' he said, wonder in his voice. 'It's Anthony I miss, not Gina. It has been all along.' He looked down at my hand, still closed over his. 'Do you read people as well as houses?'

I let go in confusion. 'I don't think so. I've only just realised I do the building thing.' I tapped the menu. 'Come on, I'm starving. What do they do nicely here?'

'Everything,' he said. 'Clare, I don't know how to thank you.'

'It hasn't worked yet,' I told him.

'It will. I'll make it. Seriously, any time you want to unburden yourself of some deeply ingrained insecurity, I'm your man, okay?'

Jonathan. My smile was possibly just a little forced as I said thank you and that I'd hold him to his word.

★　★　★

I didn't mention lunch with Ewan to my mother during our phone call that evening, but I did tell her to pass on to Dad that I'd been to the service in the cathedral and that I was joining a local choir. I also asked if she knew if there were any Woodmans in our family tree.

'I expect so,' she said helpfully. 'If you trace far enough back, everyone is related to everyone else.'

'Could you ask around? I'm curious. I think I've uncovered a local family from the past that might be distantly related. There's an image of a little girl with our colour of hair.'

'Oh,' she said, more alert. 'I will. What was her name, do you know?'

'Johanna Woodman is the grand-mother. Alys is the little girl, but she'll have married, presumably. No, forget it, Mum. It was a silly idea. It was a ridiculously long time ago.'

'Parish records, dear,' she said. 'If Alys married locally — and people really didn't move very far in historic times — it will be recorded in the church register.'

My mother is a genius.

*   *   *

On Monday I asked Leonard if I could look at the maps and plans again. As well as wanting to see the old Ely layout for myself, it had occurred to me that there might be useful snippets of family information to be gleaned from the writing in the margins.

He tutted, cross with himself. 'You're welcome to, Clare, but I still can't find the key to the chest. I know I had it . . . '

You have Mistress Johanna's gift. I remembered what the boys had said about looking for the key myself. I moistened my lips. If I really did have the same gift as Johanna, it was now or never. As I thought the words, I almost felt a sharp prod in the ribs.

I drew a breath. As Alys, I'd seen her grandmother find her neighbour's pouch. What I still didn't know was

150

exactly how she'd done it. Tentatively, I rested my hand against the wall. Just how was this going to work? I'd only ever been shown my ancestors before. Did I ask the building to see the moment when Leonard had lost his key? Presumably I only needed to look a little way into the past instead of the centuries ago that I'd been shown so far. Was it possible to fine-tune this weird ability?

A moment later I was clinging onto the wall for real. I seemed suddenly to have double vision. I saw another Leonard stride across to his long table, his arms full of documents. I saw him put the key down; saw how the papers and books already on the surface got pushed aside, moving the key towards the edge. I saw it fall noiselessly onto the carpet and bounce under the table to join the jumbled piles of books and boxes under there already.

I blinked. Heaven help me — it had worked!

'*Well done, child.*'

151

My insides turned to crushed ice at the bracing congratulations inside my mind. It was a far cry from the last time I'd heard that same voice — in a terrified hurry of thoughts, worrying about keeping 'the child' safe.

I have to keep you all safe, said Johanna Woodman with brisk acceptance, *talking across the centuries directly into my head. You, Alys, everyone. There is great danger in being unnaturally clever. People are wary of you, until they are in need. Once they have what they want, they forget your help, and only remember that you are different. This is a very ordinary gift we have, daughter, that of seeing the past; but you must be cunning and make it seem as if you are simply reasoning people's own knowledge out of them. If you see in your head where they put their lost object, keep asking them what they did next until they find it themselves. Never find something yourself. Not unless the object is your own. I will not see my family hung.*

My hand felt as if it was grafted to the wall. I pulled it away, tearing the connection with the room, with Leonard's house, with Johanna's voice. But I knew I hadn't torn anything really. The gift was fixed in me now. I didn't know whether I was grateful or terrified.

Leonard looked up from a paper he was reading. 'The maps will have to wait, Clare,' he said. 'I haven't got time to check all over this table for the key now.'

'Did it . . . ' I cleared my throat. 'Did the key fall off the table, perhaps?'

'It might have done. Search if you like, but don't disturb anything. I know where it all is, and I need it to refute this idiot who's published an entirely wrong paper. Don't these people realise the damage they do? Others read their nonsense, think it's true, use it in their arguments, and I have to waste time refuting it. Shoddy research. Very shoddy indeed. I have at least three works that would have told him at a very early stage what the truth of the matter was.'

Leonard's grey ring of hair was fluffed up, his fists balled in agitation. He really *was* upset because inaccurate information was being published. Distress came off him in waves.

In a sudden shaft of golden understanding, I knew what to say. I put aside Johanna; put aside making sense of whatever gift it was I had. Leonard's distress was in *my* world, right now, right here, and I knew how to make it better.

I spoke diffidently. 'I know you don't like the idea of other people not treating your library properly, but the very fact that it's going to be available to bona fide scholars should stop this kind of misinformation, shouldn't it?'

Leonard glanced at me, startled. I went on, thinking it out as I spoke. 'The thing is, anyone writing a paper like that from now on will be able to access the wealth of history you've built up. So if they get the facts wrong, you'll be able to shoot them down immediately, citing the texts they would have been able to access if only they'd bothered. Then they'll be discredited for lazy research and never be taken seriously again.'

'By heavens!' Leonard was so astonished by this notion that he sat down in his carved wing chair, still staring at me. Then he leapt up again, distractedly shuffling the books on the long table. 'I hadn't thought. My goodness, you're right.' He broke off, an amazing smile lighting up his face. 'You *are* right! Well I never. Well I never.'

The depth of his transformation took me aback. 'I . . . I can see the key to the chest, by the way,' I said lamely, gesturing under the table.

He waved a hand. 'Help yourself. Goodness me. What an unlooked-for benefit. This is going to save me pounds in indigestion tablets.'

I was unable to tell whether he was joking or not. He was still beaming, and

I even thought he might be *humming* under his breath. I started to smile myself, thrilled and touched that I'd found a way to reconcile Leonard to the opening up of his library.

9

I was on my way down to make a celebratory mug of tea when Ewan called me into the room on the left of the front door. This must be in the part of Almoner's Place that had originally belonged to the tiler, Master Staple.

'Clare, have you got a minute? Hamid and I are knocking up a sample bookcase for the foundation visit on Thursday. Can you check it for size and usability, please?'

'Sure,' I said. 'Hi, Hamid.'

The young chippie nodded shyly. He'd been at the pub quiz with his girlfriend, I remembered, both of them excelling at the celebrity questions.

'Hold on, I'll nip upstairs for a few random folios,' I said.

Ewan held the door open for me when I returned. 'Thought you'd like to know I emailed Anthony to say how good it was to see him over the weekend and that he and I ought to get together more often. He phoned this morning on his way to work to say he'd love to. I think it's going to be all right, Clare. Not quite as it used to be, but pretty good.' He smiled as if unable to help himself.

I beamed back. 'Fantastic. Moving on is good, isn't it?'

'It's got a lot going for it. Thanks again.'

'Don't thank me until you've heard how picky I'm going to be about your display cases,' I warned.

We played with ideas for about half an hour before I remembered I'd been about to make tea. 'Not that Leonard will notice,' I said. 'Is he going to be required at this meeting on Thursday? Do I need to prime him?'

'It's a standard review visit. I daresay you'll be getting them yourself. Newrigg are very keen on regular updates.'

'Seems fair, with the amount of money they're spending. Could be distracting, though, if they're in and out all the time.' I thought for a moment. 'I'll email suggesting I give an interim report too, shall I? Then hopefully it'll establish the routine of catching up with everything at the same time. Less disruptive to have one long visit a month than short ones at fortnightly intervals.'

'You,' said Ewan, 'are a very bright lady.'

'Only now and again,' I said, thinking of Jonathan. 'Other times I am very dumb indeed.'

★ ★ ★

My particular Newrigg Foundation director was delighted with the suggestion. Would I, he said, organise the booking of lunch nearby for the inspection party, Ewan, Leonard and myself? This would be interesting, I thought, and asked Leonard where he'd like to go. In my experience, keeping the prickliest member of a meeting comfortable was half the battle. He said he'd always been happy with the food at The Lamb Inn.

'Perfect,' I said. 'That's the one on the corner, isn't it? I'll pop down there now and book lunch straight away.'

I left before he could change his mind. I'd walked past The Lamb before, but not actually been in. The Newrigg people would like it, I thought. It had been built as a coaching inn back in the fifteenth century, and it still retained lots of lovely original features for them to revel in.

During my afternoon break, I got out the old Ely map again. I'd remembered right. No. 2 Almoner's Place had indeed belonged to the tiler, one Simon Staple by name. No. 1 had been the abode of Master John Robson; painter. Not that it mattered, really, but it was nice to put names to parts of the house.

I looked at the rest of the map. There was The Lamb on the High Street, or the 'High Rowe Strete' as it seemed to be called then. It had a lot more ground in those days. Stabling for horses would take up a fair amount of space, of course, it being a coaching inn. I wondered if I leant out of my window in Leonard's library, whether I'd see old-time carts and drays going about their business, the same way that I'd seen Johanna in the yard of No. 4 the other day. The thing was, I never had so far. Oh, I'd had feelings about the atmosphere of various buildings, and I'd been overwhelmed by emotions, but I'd never actually *seen* the past until I'd come here and connected with Almoner's Place. In fact, thinking about it some more, it could be downright awkward if I glanced out of a window and never knew *when* I was seeing. There had to be some control. I must have to deliberately want to see the past. That made sense.

★ ★ ★

Tuesday. Dinner with Mel. I mentioned it to Ewan and asked where her address was. He peered outside, where yesterday's summer weather had given way to dark clouds. 'I'll bring the car up and run you there if you like,' he said.

'I can't ask you to do that. Is there likely to be a bus?'

'It's no bother. What time?'

In the event, I was glad he'd offered, because it was pelting down by mid-afternoon. Mel rang to ask if I wanted to cancel, but I said it was okay, a colleague had offered me a lift. She immediately asked if he wanted to stay and eat too. She'd over-catered, and there was a limit to how often she could send her partner to work with curry sandwiches. I yelped with laughter and ran downstairs to find out if Ewan liked curry.

I had forgotten what fun a casual dinner with friends could be. Mel had kids, but they were both asleep by the time we turned up. Her partner Steve was that rare creature, an accountant with a sense of humour. Within minutes we'd all clicked and were talking as if we'd known each other for years.

There was only one moment when things faltered. I'd said my last job had been with Jonathan Ambergris Fine Art & Music, but that I was a library-and-early-music geek at heart, which was why I'd leapt at the Newrigg Foundation post.

Steve frowned. 'Ambergris? I'm sure I know that name. Didn't they have a scandal a few years ago? Something about selling the same old master to two different clients and then discovering it wasn't an old master at all?'

I was jolted. Surely Jonathan would never do anything like that. 'I don't know. Not while I was working for them. I kept the database of all the purchases and sales.'

'It must have been before your time then,' said Steve, and added that he'd probably remembered the details wrong anyway, although he had a feeling he'd heard that Jonathan Ambergris Fine Art & Music were sailing close to the wind again now.

The evening ended pleasantly, with a reminder about choir practice tomorrow and a spirited attempt by Mel to recruit Ewan into the group too.

'If you'd ever heard me sing, you wouldn't ask,' he said. 'This evening's been great. I've thoroughly enjoyed it. Thank you for inviting me.'

'Me too,' I said. 'I'd love to return the favour sometime. I make a reasonable spaghetti bolognese.'

'We'll sort out a date,' promised Mel. 'Childcare issues, you know.'

On the way back, I thanked Ewan again for driving me there. In an extraordinary echo of my earlier thoughts, he said on the contrary, he should thank me, as he'd forgotten the pleasure of an evening spent in a friend's home like that.

I was astonished. 'But you go out to the pub with the guys. You go home at weekends . . . '

He kept his eyes on the road, his face lit in stripes by the streetlamps, patterned by the raindrops on the side window. 'Not like this evening,' he said. 'Don't forget, I'm often away. Contractors connect with people on a project for six months or a year or whatever, then move on. Even when I was married to Gina, it was often her friends rather than mine who we went out with in the evening. And when it *was* mine, she'd sometimes get bored, and I'd be constantly trying to draw her into the conversation.' A wrinkle appeared between his eyes. 'When you mentioned your old firm, I thought I knew the name Jonathan Ambergris. I wonder if Gina and I have been to dinner with him. Has he got a big flash place in North London? Hadleigh Park or somewhere like that? Stunning wife too, if I remember. I think we went a couple of times. Always lots of guests. Puts on a magnificent spread. I'm not surprised Steve says he's strapped for cash.'

'I believe he has, yes,' I said, trying to sound offhand. 'I've never been. I know he works with a number of galleries.

Perhaps entertaining gallery managers like Gina counts as expenses.'

He did look at me then, just quickly. 'You all right?'

'Fine. I'm a bit tired, that's all.' I summoned up a smile. 'I'm not used to having a social life.' Not like Jonathan, evidently. Missing me whenever we were apart, indeed. God, I'd been a fool.

'We're nearly at Almoner's Place. You can go straight to bed and you won't even have any washing up to do. Thanks for a great evening, Clare.'

'I didn't do anything!' I protested.

'You were there. You laughed. You were interesting.' He paused. 'I'm not making a big deal of this because . . . well, just because. But I like spending time with you.' He pulled up outside No. 4, keeping the engine running, not assuming or even expecting that I'd invite him in.

'I like being with you too,' I said, appreciating his tact. 'See you tomorrow. Thanks again for the lift.'

Indoors it was quiet and peaceful, and all mine. I could almost feel my mother's disappointment from two hundred miles away, but nevertheless I slowly got ready for bed, happy to be alone, thinking about the liberating nature of friendship.

I'd enjoyed the evening. I'd enjoyed Ewan's company. Neither Mel nor Steve had treated us as if they thought we should be a couple, which was, I thought, unusual of them and very welcome.

I liked Ewan — I liked him a lot — but I was petrified of falling for someone else the way I'd fallen for Jonathan, and have to go through all that agonising, soul-ripping pain again when the relationship ended. Friendship would do me very nicely.

My phone had run out of battery at some point during the evening, so I plugged it into the bedside socket and idly watched the email count rising. Most would be junk, I suspected. Could I be bothered to check them? It was tempting not to, but if I left it until morning, there would be even more to delete.

I tapped the email icon. Junk, junk, junk, a sticky toffee pudding recipe from Mum, an automated choir reminder . . . and one from Jonathan. I stared at his name for a while before deleting the email unread.

★ ★ ★

I spent a fair amount of the next day preparing a report for the foundation, reassuring them that I was making progress with the cataloguing and the preparations for eventual user access, whilst at the same time giving them advance warning that it was going to take rather longer than they'd anticipated if we were to do it properly. After I'd finished, I went downstairs and stood in what would be the reading room, envisioning what it would look like.

'Are you having another moment?'

said Ewan from the doorway.

I grinned at him. 'No, I'm picturing what this will look like, so I can describe it to the directors tomorrow. Then they'll be happy Leonard is taking the open-to-all research seriously.'

'Stay there,' said Ewan. He came back with a computer tablet. A few swipes and a bare reading room sprang into being on the screen. 'Colour of walls?' he enquired.

'Cream. This is brilliant, Ewan.'

He shrugged modestly. 'It's games software, but I use it for buildings instead. How many tables do you want? Wooden or plastic?'

'Wood. Say six decent-sized oblong ones and a few low round ones, with comfy chairs along the wall?'

When we'd finished and saved the image, I was confident I could ask for a year's extension and we'd get it. 'Thank you,' I said.

Ewan smiled. 'We'd have had to spec it out sooner or later. Doing it at the most useful time is an hour well spent.'

'You,' I said, 'are a remarkable man. Shall we design the main display room next door as well?'

* * *

Thursday. The Newrigg Foundation directors' tour of Almoner's Place went well; they were impressed with the plans we'd put in place and approved the designs, and we adjourned amicably to The Lamb for lunch.

The finance director asked me how I was finding No. 4 as a place to live. 'I love it,' I said immediately. 'It feels exactly like home.'

'Good, good,' he said. He darted a tiny sideways look at me. 'No, ah, hitches at all? No unexplained happenings? Microwave misbehaving? Nothing falling off tables when you're nowhere near them?'

I smiled at him. 'No, it's all perfect. I'd quite like to live there forever.'

After a pause of precisely a second,

during which he calculated the amount my rent would bring in versus the likely cost of a priest, complete with bell, book and candle, he smiled genially and said he was sure that could be arranged.

When I'd made the fleeting visit to The Lamb to book lunch, I'd specified a private room if possible, but had left the choice to the manager. I hadn't looked around inside the historic coaching inn myself. Now we were shown to a pleasant oak-beamed, low-ceilinged room, which was perfect. I waited while the directors fussily decided who would sit where. I was feeling a little odd, to be honest; just slightly off-balance and out-of-step. I hoped I wasn't coming down with something, but I didn't see how I could be, as I'd felt perfectly all right during the morning. Nobody went from well to ill in a matter of seconds.

Then I worked out what the off-kilter sensation was. I was getting very faint feelings of familiarity from this place. How puzzling. Tentatively, I touched the wall next to the window.

Immediately it was as if a gauze overlay had dropped across the scene. The room was laid out differently, and — ah, yes, there was an older woman conducting a younger one through the room. Both women were dressed in what I now recognised as the daily clothing of the late 1500s, with white coifs and snowy aprons over coloured kirtles and long-sleeved cream shifts. The older woman I didn't know, but I caught the gleam of a wedding band on the younger one's finger and realised — even though her hair was now covered — that she was Alys, grown up and married to the innkeeper's son. As they passed by, her demeanour with her mother-in-law was meek and respectful; but her eyes, flashing across to the handsome curly-haired lad lounging in the doorway, danced.

I relaxed. This was a love match as well as a sound financial one, from Alys's point of view. I eased away from the wall and took my seat at the table, feeling as content as if I was Johanna herself.

Which just goes to show why you should never let down your guard. I suppose I must still have been in seeing-the-past mode as, with the excellent meal finished and enjoyed by all, we paused to look into the coffee room on our way out. Or, at least, the others looked into the coffee room. I — with my idiot hand on the door jamb — looked into a sixteenth-century parlour. A dour man in a black coif and flat black hat sat upright at an oak table, flanked by clerks. He was interviewing an elderly pinch-faced woman.

The woman stood in front of him, clearly wearing her best black kirtle and talking nineteen to the dozen. She repeatedly jabbed her finger up the road in the approximate direction of Almoner's Place. The dour man wrote on a piece of paper and pushed it across the table for the woman to make her mark. By his side, one of the clerks scribbled in a cramped fashion, dipping his pen in and out of the well. A coin changed hands. The woman smirked and scurried out.

I hadn't been aware until now that another woman stood in the shadows next to me, also watching. She hissed something at the black-clad woman as she passed, then bent down and whispered urgently into the ear of the sturdy curly-haired boy hidden by her skirts. The lad hared off in the direction of the kitchen exit.

My woman, I realised as she moved out of the shadows, was Alys's mother-in-law, but this scene was several years earlier than the one I had witnessed in the dining room. She twitched her long apron straight and picked up a tray from the side table, then schooled her face to impassivity and glided silently into the room.

'Ahem, the rest of us are leaving, Clare,' murmured Ewan as he passed.

Shaken, I fell in beside them.

10

The Newrigg directors departed for the station, well pleased with the progress of the project and the harmony of the team.

'You don't have to tell me if you don't want to,' said Ewan as he shut the front door after waving them off.

I should have known he wouldn't let the episode in The Lamb go by. I looked for a long moment into his sensible, intelligent face and took a chance on trusting him. 'Would you like to come to supper?' I asked.

'Love to,' he said promptly, 'provided there's more on offer than salad.'

I reflected that my mother would adore him.

Over the joint construction of a lasagne, I told him about every scrap of paranormal weirdness that had occurred to me since I'd arrived in

Almoner's Place. In a way it was a relief not to keep it to myself anymore. Ewan already knew about my affinity with the house, and my wall-thing, as he called it, but not how focused the gift had become.

'A gift? That's what this Johanna Woodman called it?'

I nodded. 'I'm absolutely sure she's an ancestor of mine. There's Alys's hair for a start, but also I pick up scenes involving her or Alys without even trying. For anything else, I seem to have to ask whichever building I'm in.'

A startled expression crossed his face. 'Ask the building? What, anything?'

I frowned, rubbing my forehead. 'I don't think so. I get the impression I have to have a personal reason for asking. It's not uncontrolled universal vision, thank goodness.'

'Shame. You could make a fortune working full-time for the police solving thefts and murders.'

I stared at him, aghast. Was he

serious? 'That would be horrible! I couldn't look at murders being done all the time. And suppose I saw wrong? Suppose the visions didn't come through when people were depending on me? I don't want that sort of burden.'

'If it catches a killer, though, or gives the police a lead . . . '

I put my hands over my ears. 'Stop it. I hear what you're saying, but I don't think they'd believe me, and I really don't need any more ethical decisions in my life right now.'

He stirred the cheese sauce thoughtfully. 'It might come to it one day, Clare. It's worth considering a strategy now, don't you think? But for the moment, looking at this gift another way, if you only see things connected with you or your ancestral family, it follows that the scene in the parlour of The Lamb was significant.'

'I know.' The feeling of lurking dread came back. 'I'm horribly afraid it might be witchcraft trials.'

He made the jump in an instant. 'But you said Johanna still talks to you.'

'Sort of, yes, but it's as if she talks from a fixed point in time. She lived four hundred years ago, Ewan. She could just as easily speak to me if she'd been hung or drowned as died in her bed of old age, couldn't she? I do know that's what she was afraid of.' Reluctantly, I added, 'The museum might have details of historical local trials.'

His gaze held mine. 'I'm not away this weekend, if you'd like to go to the museum together.'

* * *

In the event, the museum didn't get us any further forward. It gave us the rough period and the monies paid to informants, but no names. Of more interest was a text from Ewan's brother while we were out saying he was coming up to Cambridge to meet a client on Tuesday, and could he call in on the way back to see Ewan?

'That's fantastic,' I said.

Ewan grinned. 'Isn't it just,' he said, and texted back to say yes.

He'd already warned the lads he'd be leaving early on Tuesday, so I wasn't surprised when I heard the sound of a cab dropping someone off, followed shortly by the ping of a text for me. However, instead of a cheery message saying, 'I'm off, see you tomorrow!', it said, 'Complications.'

Complications. That sounded like a call for backup, though I couldn't imagine why Ewan of all people would need backup from me. I picked up the tray of empty mugs Leonard and I had accumulated during the morning and set off downstairs.

I didn't have to look far to find Ewan. He was in the staff kitchen, along with a slightly taller, rather more polished version of himself, and a glossy, rigorously curved, beautifully groomed woman of the kind I was very familiar with from the Jonathan days.

'Oh,' I said. 'Sorry, I didn't realise we

had visitors.' I crossed the room to the sink.

'Clare.' Ewan walked over to pull me gently next to him, his hand resting on my hip. 'Meet my brother and his wife. Anthony, Gina, this is Dr Clare Somerset.'

Complications indeed. By the dropped-jaw surprise on the faces of the others, I was the last thing they'd expected. I couldn't fault them on that. I was a little taken aback myself. Apart from anything else, where Ewan was touching me it felt as if my hip was on fire. I smiled and leaned casually against the length of his torso. That'd teach him.

'Hi,' I greeted them. 'Sorry, I can see now you aren't from the foundation. Anthony is far too like Ewan. He did mention you were popping in. I'd forgotten. I'm afraid we can't show you around because of security, but we can offer you a tea or a coffee.' By the infinitesimal relaxation in Ewan's muscles, I knew I was playing this along the right lines.

'Security?' Gina gave a sexy laugh. 'Darling, you didn't tell me I'd be on film.' She looked openly at the ceiling for a camera.

'Gina,' Ewan said pleasantly, 'is fascinated at the thought of all the old texts and manuscripts you have upstairs.'

'Oh, I am!' she said, flashing me a vivacious smile.

I beamed at her, feeling as if I was composed entirely of angles and bones compared to her designer-encased curves. 'They are wonderful. I'm very lucky to work here. You'll have to come back and browse when the reading room is up and running.'

'Can't I just have one tiny glimpse now?'

I kept my smile in place. 'I'm sorry. It's more than my job's worth to let anyone have a preview. Are you an early music fan, then? Which is your favourite period?'

'I'm interested in all art,' she said in a clipped voice. She turned to Ewan. 'Does this security of yours prevent me from using the ladies'?'

Alarm bells were ringing so loudly in my ear I was getting deafened. 'You'd better come next door and use mine,' I said. 'The one here has been taken over by the builders. You *really* don't want to experience it.'

'I don't mind roughing it. Presumably you use it.'

'Only the once,' I said, leading the way to the front door with a clear assumption that she'd follow. 'Since then, I've always gone home.'

Gina appeared to lose all interest in early music as soon as we were inside No. 4. I gritted my teeth as she wandered openly into every room in my house whilst asking unsubtle questions about how well I knew Ewan and how long our relationship had been going on for, because he'd never even mentioned the weekend before last.

'We clicked as soon as I started working here,' I said brightly, thinking any more of this and I'd have to get my smile surgically removed.

'It seems very unlike him,' she said, giving my bed a penetrating stare *en passant* as if assessing it for double occupancy. 'I've never known anyone less prone to act on impulse.'

I shrugged modestly. 'These things happen.' I comforted myself with the thought that the longer she was here with me, the more time Ewan would have with his brother.

When I eventually prised her out of my house, we met Ewan and Anthony on the doorstep.

'Oh,' said Gina gaily, 'are we off?'

'Ewan thought we'd like the café at the cathedral and a walk to the river, then he's going to run us to the station,' answered Anthony.

'What fun.' Gina turned to me. 'Are you coming?'

'I have to get back to work. You're lucky, being able to take the day off like this.'

'It was nice to meet you,' said Anthony.

'And you. Safe journey back.' I

smiled deliberately into Ewan's eyes. 'See you later.'

It could only have been five minutes before I got a surreptitious text. 'You are several kinds of wonderful.'

'I know,' I typed back.

★   ★   ★

After work, there was a ring on my doorbell. I opened the door to find Ewan with a bottle of wine and an interesting-looking box of gourmet chocolates. 'Are we still friends?' he asked.

'Come in,' I said, and led the way into the kitchen.

'Clare, I am so sorry. You were marvellous.'

'Thank you. I take it your ex-wife isn't altogether happy about the prospect of brotherly love abounding?'

'Damned if I know.' He poked disapprovingly amongst the bowl of mixed salad on the worktop. 'Where are you hiding the protein?'

'You really do have a hotline to my mother, don't you? It's in the fridge, disguised as a raised pie.'

Ewan opened the fridge door and fetched out the contents of Mum's latest red-cross parcel. 'That's more like it,' he said, getting a couple of plates down from the shelf. 'Pickle?'

I gestured wordlessly at the cupboard.

'The thing is,' he said, 'firstly, I wasn't expecting Gina at all. It was only supposed to be Anthony. Then when I saw her, I assumed like you that she was jealous about us getting together. But what floored me was how interested she was in Almoner's Place and the collection. I don't understand that at all. It really isn't her bag. She's into instant art, something she can hang on a wall and sell. Something that makes a statement. Not rare books. Not early music. And she's certainly never been so interested in my work before.'

'Maybe she's had a change of heart?'

'Not Gina. There's always something,

and it's always crucial to *her*. Last week, for example, she was talking constantly about her gallery and how her new exhibition was ruined because one of the artists had privately sold the painting that was to have had pride of place. She went on and on about how she was frantically trying to find another piece with the right 'wow' factor to placate her backers. Yet here she was today, sympathising with the difficulties of getting electricians who understood ancient buildings, agreeing about the impossibility of finding a straight edge anywhere in order to get new bookcases to fit, and sighing over the conflict between security and aesthetics. She was definitely up to something, and I don't think it was simply unsettling Anthony. When did you tell her we got together?'

It appeared we were sharing the meal. I got out wine glasses. 'I said we clicked as soon as I started working here.'

'Me too. Thank you for pretending. It

deflected her beautifully.'

'And it didn't do your standing with the pair of them any harm either.'

He darted a shamefaced look at me. 'Sorry.'

I rubbed my nose. The next bit was going to be awkward. 'Ewan, I know they're family, but I'm not sure anyone should be loose in the house while it's still in this state. Is it likely to happen again?'

'No, it damn well isn't! It shouldn't have happened today! That's why we've got the keypad on the front door and why I've trained the guys to always shut it behind them. Just the thought of all that capital upstairs behind a lock a six-year-old could open with a pair of pliers is enough to send me to the bottle. The idea was that Anthony would ring me from the station, not that they'd 'surprise' me. I was furious with Gina for putting me in such a position, but with things between Anthony and me being so shaky . . . '

I patted his arm. 'Don't worry, we

headed her off. I'm sorry she messed up your afternoon with your brother.'

'We've fixed another day next week. One for just the two of us. Anthony was as irritated as me about Gina muscling in. I don't think she's improved their marital relations any today.' He divided the pie between our plates and poured out a generous glug of wine each.

'One thing did come out of it,' I said. 'You need to allow for proper visitor toilets somewhere. I'm not going to bring every stray female back here just because I'm disinclined to have them wandering upstairs to my loo and accidentally on purpose finding the library.'

'Strangely enough, I was pencilling in WCs on my mental plan even as I was eating my cream tea. Clare — ' He broke off.

'Yes?'

'Forget work for a moment. The other day, you said something about moving on having a lot to recommend it.'

'I did. Or you did. One of us did.'

'Are you? Moving on, I mean.'

Whoa, that was perceptive. I looked at him in slight consternation. How could he tell? 'I'm working on it,' I said. 'I think I'm nearly there. Distance is quite useful as an aid to seeing how skilfully you've been taken for a ride.'

'Tell me about it.'

'I'd rather not. It'll just make me cross again.'

'I didn't mean — '

'I know.' I put out my hand and he took it. 'My . . . lover . . . caught me at exactly the right psychological moment. I was confused, overwhelmed, not very well, ready to be rescued and loved. He did tell me he was married, which was clever of him. He intimated he was about to leave his wife. He lied.'

'Bastard.'

I freed my hand again and sipped the wine. 'I won't cry if I never see him again. It's just that I'm not a hundred percent sure how I'll act if I do. It is over, honestly. It was my decision to finish things and move right away from him.' I paused. How could I tell Ewan I wasn't looking for another relationship without either hurting him or making a potentially embarrassing gaffe?

The silence had already gone on too long. I had to say something. 'I don't think I'm ready yet,' I muttered, 'but, apropos of nothing, when you rested your hand on my hip earlier, I quite liked it. I'm just telling you so you know.'

Ewan grinned. 'Just so *you* know, I liked it too.' His levity fell away. 'Clare, I'm rather keen not to do the rebound thing. Not on either side.'

I met his gaze with relief. His hazel eyes were steady. He meant it. He didn't want to go out with me until he was quite sure he wasn't smarting over Gina anymore. He didn't want me to fall into his arms as an antidote for being played for a fool by Jon. 'That seems reasonable,' I said.

He nodded. 'Good.'

We finished the meal and he stacked

the crockery neatly by the side of the sink to be washed up. His hand strayed towards the freezer.

'If you're after ice-cream,' I said, 'there isn't any. I forgot to buy some.'

'The pie made up for it,' he said, putting on a brave face. 'I might have a scraping of sorbet left in my tub at home.'

'You put empty tubs back in your freezer?' I asked.

'You never know when the dessert fairy might come visiting. She never has yet, but that doesn't stop me hoping.'

I chuckled and followed him to the door, watching as he lifted his jacket down from one of the hooks. It was lovely sharing meals with Ewan. He fitted nicely into the house. He didn't crowd me. Out of nowhere, the feeling of his hand resting on my hip came back to me, along with an overwhelming loneliness. I cleared my throat. 'Not rebounding at all, but we could, perhaps, have one kiss on account?'

He half-turned with his hand on the

latch and gave me that slow smile. 'On account of what?'

'On account of I'd quite like a kiss.'

'Well, now you mention it . . . ' He bent his head to my upturned face. Then he curved an arm around my waist with satisfactory firmness, brushed his mouth against mine . . . and before we knew it, we were lifetime-deep in a proper first kiss. It was a revelation. Nobody, *nobody*, had ever kissed me like this before. I dissolved and reformed. I felt myself unfurl. I came alive.

'Wow,' I said when we eventually drew apart. 'That was . . . um . . . yeah. I'll, um, get on with the non-rebounding issue straight away.'

'Good plan,' he said, his breathing ragged. 'Me too. Christ, Clare . . . ' He passed a hand across his face. 'I'll, ah, see you tomorrow. I've . . . I've got accounts to do. Cold showers to take. That sort of thing.'

So much for just being friends. At least Ewan was as shaken as me. Why was my life not ever cut and dried?

Alone again, I started looking up parish records for Alys and her innkeeper on the internet, but Ewan's kiss lingered on my lips, making concentration difficult. Besides, I had a feeling I was looking in the wrong place. If I wanted to see whether Johanna had made it to her granddaughter's wedding day, I probably ought to be leaning against the wall of the parish church of St Mary.

* * *

The next day everything was, superficially at least, back to normal. I deleted an unread email from Jonathan in the morning. I bantered gently with Ewan a couple of times during the day (with my lips twitching the entire time). I went to choir in the evening. I slept dreamlessly. Only the supermarket delivery van turning up at midday with two separate orders of a single tub of ice-cream apparently sent from a 'Mr Des

Sertfayre' and 'Ms Dess Urtfairi', one for me and one for Ewan, was in any way out of the ordinary.

'Thank you,' I said, passing him on the stairs later, feeling slightly overfull with salted caramel.

'How did you know I liked double chocolate?' he asked.

'No man buys a woman interesting boxes of chocolates without a thorough working knowledge of the subject himself. Besides, they were out of vanilla.'

*   *   *

On Thursday, Leonard was off to a sale. 'Are you allowed to?' I asked.

He looked at me frostily. 'Provided I stay within budget and you catalogue it as soon as I get back.'

I grinned. 'Enjoy yourself.'

No sooner had he left Almoner's Place than Jonathan rang. Despite everything, my heart still did a flip when I saw his name on the display. I suppose five years of conditioning does take longer than a fortnight to get over. 'Shush,' I told the warbling phone. 'It's over.' The phone continued to ring. I stiffened my spine and pressed the 'block' icon.

An hour later I got another call. 'Clare Somerset,' I answered, not recognising the number on the display.

'Clare, thank goodness. You haven't been answering me, you're ignoring my emails and you sounded *so* distraught the other day. I've been terribly worried about you.'

He'd borrowed someone else's phone! I couldn't believe it. I hardened my heart. 'Hello, Jonathan. There's an easy solution, you know. If you'd only stop emailing and phoning me, I wouldn't need to not answer you. Then you'd have no cause to worry.'

'Clare, darling, I still care about you.'

'Then leave me alone.' I heard my voice rise and tried to moderate it. 'We are finished, Jon. It's not fair on me for you to keep trying. I'm busy, I'm loving my job here, and I'm perfectly well. I can't imagine why you think I might not be. You've got your life, and I've got mine, and I'm doing my level best to make them both work. You're the one trying to derail things and I wish you'd stop. I'm sorry, Jonathan, but I don't know how much clearer I can be. Give the phone back to whoever you borrowed it from and don't ring me again.' I jabbed the 'off' button and, just for good measure, blocked that number too before blotting my eyes with a tissue.

'Problems?'

I looked up to see Ewan in the doorway of the library. He was leaning easily against the door jamb, ready to either continue wherever he was going or come in and sympathise as I wanted. I fought the impulse to burrow into his arms for a comforting hug. 'Yes, as you probably heard.'

'I did a bit.'

I stood up. 'I think I need more tea.'

He fell into step beside me. 'Jonathan,'

he mused aloud. 'Would that be . . . ?'

'Yes,' I said shortly. 'Yes, Jonathan Ambergris. You now know everything.'

'He sounded,' said Ewan thoughtfully, 'like a bit of a prick.'

I was startled into a half-laugh, half-sob. 'He's certainly behaving like one at the moment. It doesn't make it any easier, knowing you've been having an affair with an idiot.'

Ewan dropped a light kiss on my hair. 'We've all done stupid things in our time. You are talking to the man who was married to Gina for six years. Want a flapjack?'

I blew my nose. 'Yes, please. Was that a kiss?'

'Just a friendly one.'

'Okay.'

11

Leonard, it transpired, had been successful at the auction. He spent the afternoon gloating over his new treasure, reluctantly letting the manuscript out of his hands just long enough for me to admire it, hear all about its provenance, and catalogue it.

'The collectors were out in force, naturally,' he said. 'I left them to mop up the other items. More fool them if they spend their budgets before the big sale next week. This was the item I wanted.'

I smiled at him. 'Then I'm glad you got it. There you are, all done. I just need a paragraph of description, please.'

He rattled me off a couple of concise sentences. 'Jonathan Ambergris was there,' he added as an afterthought. 'Spending over the odds as usual. He asked how you were getting on. I said I had no complaints.'

I was jolted, but covered it up. 'Leonard, you fibber. You're always complaining.'

'Not,' he said loftily, 'about you.'

'Thank you,' I said, touched.

He bore his prize away, leaving me with conflicting thoughts. So Jonathan had actually been at the sale or on his way to it when he rang me this morning. That made me uneasy. He was usually completely focused on one thing at one time. I had gone with him to sales sometimes. On the way there, I might not have existed, as all his attention was geared towards the lot he was interested in. It was only on the way back that he would relax. If he'd now let personal business distract him from work, did that mean he really was missing me? Was that why he kept trying to contact me? I didn't know what to think anymore.

Maybe Jonathan had actually listened to me this time. At any rate, there were no further calls or emails from him. I put him out of my mind and got on with my life. Walking back from the quiz through the Friday night dusk, Ewan asked what I was doing over the weekend.

'I thought I'd try the St Mary's parish registers to see if I can find any trace of Alys getting married. It was Mum's idea. What about you? Going home?'

It wasn't too dark to see the old-fashioned look he directed at me. 'Not a chance. Gina and Anthony have been news-spreading. The moment I walk through the door, I'm toast. Mum won't let me move from the spot until I've told her all about you.'

'Oops,' I said. 'Do you mind?'

He cleared his throat. 'I don't mind not going back this weekend,' he said. 'I'm beginning to mind it not being true about you and me.'

For a split-second my heart stopped. I rather thought my bones might have melted as well. 'You could come in now

for a coffee,' I managed. 'We could
. . . talk about it. And maybe have
another kiss on account.'

He didn't look at me, but there was a
smile on his lips. 'On account of what?'

'On account of I really enjoyed the
last one.'

He put his arm around my shoulders.
I made the tiniest inarticulate sound
and my bones melted a little more. I felt
. . . I don't know. In the words of the
harvest hymn, I felt safely gathered in.

'Me too,' he said.

For all the laid-back quality of his
approach, we'd barely got the door shut
before I was twisting blissfully into his
embrace.

'Oh,' I said breathlessly as soon as I
could talk again. 'I've been missing this
ever since we said goodbye on Tuesday.'

'You're not the only one. How's the
rebounding?'

'I'm over it. Totally.'

'Hmmm, you're forgetting I heard
the phone call. I'm still not going to
rush things.'

'Damn. So I should make that coffee?'

'Probably.'

We went through to the kitchen. I turned around from filling the kettle to see Ewan peering inside the fridge.

'Ewan, you cannot be hungry. Not after the fish and chips.'

'I'm looking to see what I need to bring over if we are going to cook a nice meal together tomorrow night.'

A warm glow lodged in my chest. Ewan might not be rushing things, but we appeared to have moved seamlessly into the stage Granny used to refer to as walking out. 'That sounds promising,' I said.

'Although now you come to mention it, a morsel of cheese and biscuits now wouldn't go amiss.'

'The brie does need eating up,' I said with a straight face.

'I noticed.' He busied himself with plates and cheese knives. 'These parish records, are they the sort of thing that take a lot of time?'

'Almost certainly,' I said. 'Historic handwriting and the vagaries of sixteenth-century spelling being what they are.'

'Oh.'

I relented. 'On the other hand, I'm going to be in Ely for at least a year, so I could simply touch base with the vicar, mention that Dad is in the trade, and set up visiting rights for lunch-times. Did you have something else in mind for tomorrow, then?'

Ewan's face became animated. 'It's just that there's a drainage museum at Prickwillow, and these places are so much better when you have someone else to go with.'

I looked at him carefully to see whether he was joking. It seemed he wasn't. I cut myself a piece of brie and balanced it on a wholemeal biscuit. 'Walking out with you is going to be a whole new voyage of discovery,' I remarked.

'Walking out,' he said, rolling the phrase around his tongue. 'I like it.'

* * *

I still hadn't done the cathedral tour, so in revenge for the drainage museum (which had actually been fascinating), we went around it on Sunday afternoon.

'I met Mel for coffee this morning,' I said. 'She and Steve have a window of opportunity for dinner out with friends on Tuesday, due to Steve's mum announcing an unexpected visit and thereby letting herself in for babysitting duties, so I invited them over. Would you like to come? Or will you still be busy with Anthony?'

'I won't be busy with him at all on Tuesday,' said Ewan. 'Gina has an event that she needs him to accompany her to, so we've changed the day.' He smiled placidly. 'There are many things I don't miss at all about life with Gina.'

I put on a contrite face. 'I didn't realise you were averse to socialising. You don't have to come to dinner with Mel and Steve.'

'I'm only averse to socialising with arty types while wearing a dicky-bow.

Friends are a different matter entirely. Besides, you promised spaghetti bolognese.'

*   *   *

I still wanted to find out about Johanna and Alys, so I started going to St Mary's at lunchtimes to work my way through the 1570s parish registers.

'We're missing you in the kitchen this week,' said Ewan on Thursday morning. 'Can't you take a shortcut and do the wall thing?'

I grinned at him. 'I've tried. I can't get the focus. Too much history. Too many weddings and funerals. Hundreds of years of parish past. Anyway, you're out yourself today. Isn't Anthony coming over?'

'Yes, only for a quick lunch on his way to see a client. I told him it wasn't worth bothering; but Gina, of all people, said he mustn't disappoint me. Are personality transplants a thing, do you know?'

'You can never tell with medical

science,' I said. 'Have a nice time.' And I ran upstairs to make sure Leonard had everything he needed for today's sale of rare books in Bury St Edmunds.

Unfortunately, when I got to St Mary's later, the vicar apologetically told me he had a wedding rehearsal and the bride's mother had taken over the vestry. 'No matter,' I said. 'I'll come back tomorrow.' I debated going down to the river to eat my sandwich, but as it was market day, I returned straight to Almoner's Place via the market and a fresh loaf of olive bread.

Hamid was hovering in the hallway. He looked relieved to see me. 'Your visitor is here already, Clare. He is upstairs.'

I stopped. 'My visitor?'

'Yes. He apologised for being so very early and said he was happy to do some work in the library while he waited for you.'

I felt a stab of alarm. Oh, dear Lord, it must be a Newrigg director and I'd missed an email. He'd be here to check up on something and had now been presented with a great gaping hole in our security. 'He's in the library?'

I hadn't even thought! I should never have gone out at the same time as Ewan on a day when Leonard was away too. *Anyone* could have walked in and even now be wreaking havoc amongst the treasures. One of us ought to always be here to safeguard them.

'Thank you, Hamid,' I said, because it wasn't his fault. He hadn't been properly briefed. Inwardly planning new security measures, I hurried upstairs.

The library door was open. I slipped inside. And stopped with an enormous thud of my heart. A fair-haired man sat at one of the occasional tables, gently turning the leaves of a twelfth-century illuminated text. He was handling it with reverence and awe, his long fingers lingering on the pages the way they used to linger on my skin.

My visitor wasn't a Newrigg director. It was Jonathan.

I swear my legs would have given way had I not had the doorpost for support. Putting Jon out of my mind, blocking his number and deleting his emails had been easy compared to resisting the immense *whumph* of emotion I got from seeing him again in the flesh. My fingers pressed into the plaster of the wall as I willed myself to stay vertical. What was he doing here? I *so* did not need this.

Jon gave a slight start. He swivelled in the chair, coming upright at the same time. His eyes warmed. 'Clare, I've missed you so much.' He took a few steps forward, arms outstretched.

No, I thought, but my treacherous body was already preparing for the embrace, already fabricating a cosy scenario where I'd believe Jon's lies about it all being a mistake, that he loved me, that everything would be all right.

No, I thought again fiercely, and willed Marianne's joyful face to mind. Damn Ewan. Why hadn't he taken me

off to bed as soon as we'd kissed that
first time, so I'd have other memories
by now to smother the ones of
Jonathan?

'No,' I said out loud, and immediately answered myself. Because he was
Ewan, of course. Ewan would never
take the easy option of a rebound
romance. He was a long-haul pilot if
ever there was one; and, given the rich,
complex, sensational nature of his
kisses, it wasn't a journey I was going to
get tired of any time soon.

I smiled broadly. 'No,' I said again,
remembering those kisses now, the feel
of them on my lips, the taking-me-
seriously look on his face, the pledge
of a far better future for us in all
the things he didn't say, than any
temporary high Jon's fancy words
might have promised. The thought of
Ewan filled me with strength. He was
like a long drink of ice-cold mountain
water on a temperate day. Jon was a
surreptitious sip of forbidden cocktail,
hastily replaced on the table before

anyone noticed it was missing.

'You shouldn't be here, Jon,' I said. 'I'm going to have to show you out. Sorry.'

Jonathan was still walking towards me, still with his arms outstretched. 'Darling,' he said, half-laughing. 'I just wanted to see you. I want to stay friends, Clare, even though you've found someone else. We've been so much to each other. We can't just stop.'

'Yes, we can,' I said, and tried to think of a cliché he'd relate to. 'We are ships that have passed in the night. Morning might have taken a while to dawn, but it's here now. You go your way. I'll go mine.'

He stopped and looked at me tenderly. 'Are you sure, Clare?'

I nodded. 'I'm sure.'

He spread his hands in a graceful gesture. 'So be it. I had to try one last time, face to face. You're a very special person, you know.' He bent to pick up his briefcase.

Just like that? Perversely, prickles of

anxiety chased across my skin. Surely that was too easy. Would Jonathan really have come all this way without an ulterior motive, just to have me tell him what I'd already said half a dozen times on the phone? What was he up to? Was he going to grab me? Force a kiss on me in the hopes I'd fall helplessly back in love with him? But no, he had his case in one hand and his coat over the other arm. He was going to walk straight past me, still talking in that lightly regretful voice . . .

Alarm bells were clamouring even louder than when I was worried about Gina. *What am I missing? What am I missing? What am I missing?*

My fingernails were still digging into the plaster of the wall as the question screamed through my head. What *was* I missing? There had to be something. And then I nearly screamed for real as *another* Jonathan, identically dressed, strode past my shoulder, coming into the room from the doorway behind me. He rotated, staring around the library with a look of triumph. Keeping one eye on the door, he swiftly crossed to different parts of the room, running his fingers across spines and plucking two large folios from crowded bookshelves before scooping up a superb illustrated madrigal I had only this morning catalogued. He put them all in his case and was just assessing the bays ready for a fourth object when his head went up as if he'd heard something downstairs. Fury passed over his face. He sat smoothly at the table where I'd seen him on first entering the library, all his attention on the manuscript in front of him.

For a moment I was dizzy, seeing two of them in front of me, then the ghost-Jon was gone, vanished back into the past.

I stood there, glued to the wall, only just keeping the horror of what I had witnessed at bay. Jonathan was still talking. The flashback had taken no time at all.

' . . . You're a very special person, Clare.'

'So special,' I said, not recognising my own voice, 'that you thought nothing of stealing five years of my life. You had no intention ever of leaving Marianne, but you wanted me as well. And now you're using me again.'

'I just wanted to see you, darling. You're looking sensational. Academic life must suit you. I know you're right and I *should* try to forget you. God knows it won't be easy.'

'Why aren't you at the Bury St Edmunds sale, Jonathan? Not like you to miss one. Is the purse running low? Or is it because you know Leonard will be there? There, as in specifically *not here*. And how strange that you should show up at lunchtime when you know I'm not likely to be on the premises either.'

Nor was Ewan. The significance of that hit me like a shower of ice. Normally he'd be eating downstairs, but Anthony had changed the date of their meeting because Gina asked him to. Gina, who managed a gallery for which she had an urgent need of a statement piece.

Nausea rose to my throat. I held it there. 'Put them back, Jonathan,' I said.

An unguarded emotion flashed across his face: fear, swiftly followed by bluff. 'Whatever are you talking about, Clare?'

'You heard,' I said. 'Take the three items you have stolen from this collection out of your briefcase and put them on the chair.' I got my phone out of my pocket with shaking fingers. 'The longer you take to do it, the longer I'll have to call the police.'

'Clare!'

I met his hurt gaze, blazingly angry now, and furiously, furiously ashamed of myself for behaving in such a way in the past that had led him to believe I'd turn a blind eye to his thievery now. 'Three items, Jonathan.'

'I should have known the ludicrous lack of security was a blind,' said Jonathan, getting two large books and a small one out of his briefcase.

I cast them a rapid glance. 'It's very

kind of you to leave Leonard your latest acquisition, but I believe he would prefer his madrigal.'

'You cannot know that!' Jon looked angrily around the room for a camera.

'The madrigal, Jon. I realise the sale of it would pay your mortgage for a year, but somehow I can't quite bring myself to care.'

He put it on the table with bad grace, replacing it in his bag with the small book that didn't match my vision of anything he'd taken. 'You report this and I'll maintain we were in collusion.'

'As long as you get out of my life now, I won't say anything. I'll stay here in obscurity and neither of us will bother the other again. Don't kid yourself it's because I still have any feelings for you. I'm doing this for Marianne and the children. I'm choosing to believe you were overcome by the temptation of the moment, not that you deliberately targeted Almoner's Place on a day you knew Leonard would be away, because you are in deep financial trouble.'

He walked past me towards the door. 'Just out of interest, where is the surveillance? I understood there wasn't any.'

I laughed. 'Jonathan, you don't seriously think we'd have all this stock and nothing keeping watch over it? You also don't seriously think I would *tell* people about it?'

'I admit it seemed unlikely, but . . . '

'Just go. I don't want to see you ever again. And if you want some free fiscal advice, then I'd say as a general rule it's safer to cut back on the lifestyle than to steal. You could give fewer parties, perhaps. Not keep so many pied-à-terres in the City.' I held his eyes deliberately. 'And maybe it would be wise to cut down on the promises to galleries in exchange for services rendered.'

I saw a momentary gleam of respect in his eyes. It might have been the first in all the time I'd known him. He saluted me lazily and walked out of the door.

Ewan detached himself from the wall of the passageway in silence and strolled after us. My eyes widened, though I didn't shift my attention from Jonathan. How long had Ewan been there? Not that it mattered. I was enormously grateful for the support now.

On the doorstep, Jon said, 'I suppose a goodbye kiss is out of the question?' He looked past me to Ewan and dropped his voice. 'Ah. Inappropriate. Well, I hope you'll be very happy. No bones broken, eh? You can't blame me for trying.'

I regarded him coldly. 'Can I not? Who did you think was going to get the blame when the items were found to be missing? You must hate me very much for daring to leave you.'

He almost looked rueful. 'On the contrary, Clare. I have never admired you more.' Then he turned and walked away.

'I don't think,' said Ewan meditatively behind me, 'that I'd have let him go that easily, had it been me.'

'I couldn't do anything else,' I said. 'There was no evidence bar mine, and that came from the gift. I'd have come off the worse, believe me. He'd say it was collusion, and that I was saving him from bankruptcy or something and that I was hoping to reestablish our relationship. As it is, I've recovered the items, and I'm pretty sure he'll never willingly see me again. How long had you been there?'

'Not for the whole time, just enough to catch the drift and to see you had the situation in hand. If he'd laid a finger on you, I would have been happy to pulverise him first and ask questions afterwards.'

I leaned against him, very wobbly now it was over. 'And have him sue you for assault. That's my boy.' I swallowed. 'I saw him, Ewan. It was horrible. I'd finally got him to admit we were finished. He was just about to leave, but it was too easy. I knew I was missing something and I couldn't think what it might be. I squeezed against the wall to give him space to get past — I think I was actually gripping the wall . . . and then the library showed me him *taking the manuscripts*. But it only showed me right at the last moment! What if it hadn't? What if he'd walked out with them?'

Ewan held me close and safe, wrapping me in security. My cheek was pressed against the cotton of his T-shirt. I could smell the faint coconut-and-honey scent of his soap. 'No chance. After that crack he made about a goodbye kiss, I was ready to take him apart on principle. He wouldn't have got away with anything.'

I remembered something else. 'Oh. Ewan, this is really important. I hate to say it, but I think Jonathan must have got his information from Gina. He said he wanted to stay friends *even though I'd found someone else*. Nobody but Gina could have told him that.'

'Damn,' said Ewan quietly. Then he sighed. 'I hope it was in exchange for favours for the gallery, not as payment for anything else she might have let herself in for. Was that what you meant about 'services rendered'?'

'Yes. You said she was looking for a special piece urgently for the gallery, didn't you? She'd have asked everywhere. Jonathan has crib sheets on everyone he deals with. He could easily have agreed, provided she did a little light reconnaissance for him. Can you send her a carefully worded email?'

'I shall send both her and Anthony an amusing account of the dressing-down I got from Newrigg for leaving Almoner's Place untended while I met Anthony, adding that fortunately no harm was done as the surveillance systems held up. Would you like a mug of tea?'

'A bucketful, please. And much as she isn't my favourite person, I think I will say something to Gina next time I meet her. An unbuttoned girly talk in the ladies', perhaps, on the dangers of trusting smooth-talking arts dealers.'

'Thank you,' said Ewan. 'He's right about one thing. You are pretty special.'

12

All through the afternoon, I kept getting horrible shivers about how very, very lucky we had been. Suppose I hadn't come back early from lunch? Suppose I hadn't inherited Johanna's gift? Suppose I hadn't used it?

When I paused before Ewan's open door at the end of the afternoon, thinking I'd ask if he wanted a drink or anything, or perhaps just if he wanted to spend the evening in a mutual hug, his screen was crammed with windows showing comparisons between various security systems.

My blood turned even colder as my understanding suddenly updated itself. If Jonathan had got away with his heist, it wouldn't have just been my job on the line. Ewan, as site manager, could have had his whole career severely compromised. He was in charge, after all. A theft of this magnitude could crucify him.

And yet he had trusted me to deal with Jonathan. He hadn't waded in and taken over. I didn't know any other man in the world who would have stood by — albeit watchfully — and let me do the right thing.

Love. It hit me without warning; drenched me from head to toe. I loved this man with all my heart. There had to be something I could do for him in return. It needed to be something difficult. Something that only I could do. I gazed around the hallway, seeking inspiration.

'I know you're standing there,' said Ewan without turning around. 'Come in and have a look at these. I'm going to make every last inch of this place secure if I have to pay for the blasted kit myself.'

And then it came to me — the priest hole in the kitchen of No. 3. Ewan had been disappointed that I hadn't wanted to go into the hidden room properly so

I could date it for him. The truth was, I'd been slammed with such terrible sorrow when we discovered it that I couldn't bear the thought of putting myself through the experience again. How utterly pathetic and selfish of me. With the old kitchen being turned into a communal rest room for the researchers, I wasn't going to be able to ignore it forever, was I? The time to do something about it was right now.

'In a minute,' I said. 'You come with me first.'

He put his pen down and stood up. His eyes were tired, his stance weary. I recognised at the back of his eyes the stalking horror of what might have been. 'You're looking very determined,' he said.

I raised myself on tiptoe and kissed his cheek. His arm came automatically around my waist. 'I thought,' I said, 'in view of lunchtime, that I'd give you a present.'

He grinned. 'Give me a few minutes to lock up, then.'

I slapped his arm lightly. 'Not that sort of present. And honestly, it's not much of one, but I think you'll like it. Come with me.'

I led him through the reading room and down to the old kitchen. It had been mostly cleared of stores now, so I took a deep breath, then walked directly into the alcove cupboard. The false wall was standing open at the far end.

'Clare,' said Ewan, following me, 'you don't have to do this.'

I smiled at him over my shoulder. 'Yes, I do. You want it dated. I want whatever it is laid to rest. I can have a stab at the date if nothing else.'

He pulled me back. 'You don't. I love you already. You don't have to prove anything.'

'You love me?'

He pulled me closer. 'Yes, yes of course I do. So let's lock up and go home.'

'I love you too. Which is exactly why I have to do this. Do you realise how horribly wrong everything could have gone at lunchtime?'

'It was never going to go wrong. We're a good team.'

'Hindsight,' I said, 'is a wonderful thing.' I kissed him briefly on the lips and stepped around the secret door.

'Idiot,' he said with a chuckle, and came in after me.

I braced myself against the fear, flexed my hand just once, and put it flat against the real end wall.

At once I realised the wall was connected to the corner of my own house next door. The discovery was such a comfort — bringing with it the feelings of love and warmth I associated with No. 4 — that it distracted me from the sorrow around me and jumped my mind much further than I'd expected. There were no priests here, either Protestant or Catholic. Instead, to my utter astonishment, I saw Johanna Woodman. *My* Johanna from *my* house. The shock of it took my breath away.

'It's Johanna,' I said aloud. 'Ewan, it's

my Johanna, and she's okay.' I felt his hand take mine, but it was too remote from my vision to distract me.

Johanna sat composedly on a narrow bed, upright and busy, darning hose by the light of a candle. Her coif was smooth against her head, her clothes neat and unwrinkled, her movements unhurried. I frowned, working out that she was unaware of me. I was seeing an event in the past, like I had in the library, like I had in my lounge, not interacting with her spirit presence.

The sorrow had been hers, I learnt. That was why it had felt familiar. Sorrow that events should have come to this. That her own neighbour should have called her a witch. The charge had been made from spite, rescinded within the week. It was well known that the accuser, Mistress Staple from No. 2, harboured a grudge against the Wood-mans due to Johanna's oldest son Thomas not making a match with their daughter.

All the same, inquisitors are as

hungry as the next man; and on the grounds that a hungry man will rarely leave a faggot to smoulder when there is profit to be had from a fire, Johanna had prudently announced an immediate visit to her married daughter in Norwich. It was a goodly distance, and the supposed trip would serve as an excuse for her absence until the inquisitors had moved on. In reality, she had moved into the stonemason's hidden room next door in No. 3, where she could keep a watchful eye on her household and continue to be useful to them until the witchfinders had departed to spread fear through the next luckless town.

With her out of sight, she hoped any neighbourhood interest would die down, and those with long memories would forget that her own great-aunt had once also had the finding gift. Johanna didn't want anyone to ruminate on bloodlines and start to investigate Alys. The child was coming along, but was such a ball of bright chatter that any indiscretions could have consequences.

Being an entirely practical woman, the thought was also in Johanna's mind that by the time she 'returned', her neighbours might have remembered how much more useful she was to them alive than hanged or imprisoned.

'Clare,' said Ewan, shaking me gently. 'Clare, are you all right?'

I took my hand stiffly off the wall. I understood now. An affinity with buildings was an occasional family talent. It was my coming to the original family house that had crystallised my gift. I'd always had it, but being in a place with such a strong connection to me — even though I doubted I'd ever know my exact family tree — focused and sharpened it. Johanna and I had the same ability. We saw the history of the spaces that buildings enclosed. In Johanna's time, Almoner's Place and its neighbours were new, so there was only recent history, which was why she used the gift mostly to find lost things. I had been so confused and overwhelmed in Italy because there was so much more of the past available, held suspended in the memory fabric of the walls.

As for when I'd felt Johanna Woodman's thoughts on Palace Green and in the old gaol, that was simply a testament to the power of my redoubtable ancestor's fierce need to protect others in her family who possessed the same 'ordinary gift'. I sent her a respectful salute across the centuries. Peace came to me, unexpected and reassuring. I smiled at Ewan. I might even have laughed softly. The gift had been bestowed upon me to use, so use it I would. It was my duty now, and my burden.

'Yes,' I said. 'Yes, I'm very much all right.'

Ewan smiled and traced the side of my face with his hand. 'You don't have to tell me about it if you don't want to,' he said.

I moved closer to him and put my arms around his neck. He held me close. Gathered in. 'I love you,' I said.

'And I love you.' He brushed my lips with his.

'I do want to tell you about Johanna, but it might take awhile.'

'All night?' he said on a whisper of breath.

'Easily,' I said.

He gave me a lingering, full-of-promise kiss and then stepped back. 'In that case, we'll need dinner first. Your place or mine?'

'Mine,' I said, because No. 4 was mine and I belonged there, now and forever, and Ewan and I were both ready.

Also, being in my own way just as practical as Johanna, I decided that my house was a lot handier for work tomorrow morning for the pair of us than his was.

We do hope that you have enjoyed reading this large print book.

Did you know that all of our titles are available for purchase?

We publish a wide range of high quality large print books including:
Romances, Mysteries, Classics
General Fiction
Non Fiction and Westerns

Special interest titles available in large print are:
The Little Oxford Dictionary
Music Book, Song Book
Hymn Book, Service Book

Also available from us courtesy of Oxford University Press:
Young Readers' Dictionary
(large print edition)
Young Readers' Thesaurus
(large print edition)

For further information or a free brochure, please contact us at:
Ulverscroft Large Print Books Ltd.,
The Green, Bradgate Road, Anstey,
Leicester, LE7 7FU, England.
Tel: (00 44) **0116 236 4325**
Fax: (00 44) **0116 234 0205**

Other titles in the
Linford Romance Library:

LADY EMMA'S REVENGE

Fenella J. Miller

Lady Emma Stanton is determined to discover who killed her husband, even if it means enlisting the assistance of a Bow Street Runner. Sergeant Samuel Ross is no gentleman; he has rough manners and little time for etiquette. So when Emma and Sam decide the best way to ferret out the criminal is to pose as husband and wife, they are quite the mismatched pair. Soon, each discovers they have growing feelings for the other — but an intimate relationship across such a social divide is out of the question . . .

STANDING THE TEST OF TIME

Sarah Purdue

When Grace Taylor wins a scholarship to study music at the exclusive Henry Tyndale School, she is determined to work hard to realise her dream of becoming a professional musician. There she meets the charming young Adam, and it feels like they were meant for each other — until a vicious bully with a wealthy father, to whom the school is beholden, succeeds in breaking them apart . . . Eight years later, fate throws Grace and Adam together again. Can they overcome the shadows of the past and make a life together?

EYE OF THE STORM

Sally Quilford

When Nadine Middleton travels to Egypt, she does not expect to meet Lancaster Smith, the man who discredited her father. As she embarks on a quest to clear Raleigh Middleton's name, she wonders who is friend and who is foe amongst the other passengers on the Nile steamer. With one apparent death and another person going missing, along with some mind-blowing and life-threatening riddles to solve, Nadine finds herself relying on Lancaster more and more — but can she trust him?

PARTHENA'S PROMISE

Valerie Holmes

1815: Parthena arrives in a small Yorkshire village to take up a post as governess, only to find that the family has moved away, leaving her stranded on her own in an unfamiliar place. Here she meets Jerome Fender, a soldier returning from the wars. He is enchanted by Thena and offers to help her. Full of desperation, however, she 'borrows' his money, shouting a promise to pay him back as she flees. Incensed, Jerome vows to find her and get his money back — as well as an explanation . . .